Geoff Cochrane is the author of numerous highly regarded collections of poems and two novels. In 2009 he was awarded the Janet Frame Prize for Poetry, and in 2010 the inaugural Nigel Cox Unity Books Award. *Astonished Dice* collects his two slim volumes of short stories, originally published in limited editions, the early novella 'Quest Clinic', and more recent stories.

'One exits so many slim volumes with slim pickings. Then there are those books of poetry that seem fuller than fiction. Geoff Cochrane's is a whole world, rendered in lines at once compressed and open, mysterious and approachable. These are poems of great formal poise and terrific candour.'

Damien Wilkins on *Vanilla Wine*

'It becomes apparent that Cochrane is not merely a frugal poet, thriftily recycling anecdotal skerricks and wisps of philosophical thoughts and self-destructive deeds into highly crafted and sophisticated works of art, but also a darkly humorous memorialist: a keeper of the keys for marginal Wellington.'

David Eggleton on *84-484*

Also by Geoff Cochrane

Poetry
Images of Midnight City
The Sea the Landsman Knows
Taming the Smoke
Kandinsky's Mirror
Aztec Noon: Poems 1976–1992
Into India
Acetylene
Nine Poems
Vanilla Wine
Hypnic Jerks
84-484
Pocket Edition
The Worm in the Tequila
The Bengal Engine's Mango Afterglow

Novels
Tin Nimbus
Blood

Short Stories
Brindle Embers
White Nights

ASTONISHED DICE

Geoff Cochrane

Victoria University Press

VICTORIA UNIVERSITY PRESS
Victoria University of Wellington
PO Box 600 Wellington
vup.victoria.ac.nz

National Library of New Zealand Cataloguing-in-Publication Data

Cochrane, Geoff, 1951-
Astonished dice : collected short stories / Geoff Cochrane.
ISBN 978-0-86473-921-6
I. Title
NZ823.2—dc 23

Printed by Printstop, Wellington

For my family, friends and fans,
and in memory of Gerry Melling

Penguins topple like astonished dice.
Anne Carson

Contents

3. WHITE NIGHTS

4.

Acknowledgements

These stories were first published as follows:

Brindle Embers, Thumbprint press, 2002. *White Nights*, Thumbprint Press, 2004. 'Movie', 'A Winter's Tale', 'Apex Landscaping', *Sport 31*, 2003. 'Down Through the Pines', 'Sacraments', 'Tattoo', *Sport 33*, 2005. 'Little Steps', *Sport 8*, 1992. 'Quest Clinic', *Sport 9*, 1992.

1

Movie

He had a room, and that was all-important.

He had a room and red typewriter and a plastic daffodil in a Fanta bottle.

Times had changed, and one must have a base.

He'd breakfast on cigarettes and cheap port.

As the days and weeks went by, the glass from which he drank got more and more sticky, besmirched. Began to look rusty, brownly bloody, as if stained by ancient gore.

On steel-bright, fragrant mornings, he'd open his door and survey the scene without.

Cowpats of concrete. Crude, tilting, asymmetrical steps.

Men had died on those steps. Drunkards had broken their necks on those steps.

His name was Joel Stella.

One of the few books he owned was Samuel Beckett's *First Love*.

When winter came, he sat at his red typewriter and

worked on his screenplay. It was all about rain and night, the dismaying sweetness of light on sodden asphalt.

Walking the wet streets, he planned elaborate tracking shots.

His movie would incorporate the music of Steely Dan and Neil Young.

Of course, the filming of his script was never more than the most remote possibility. Like winning a huge sum of money, say.

Lying in water green and curry-hot, he dreamed a snowy, piney version of China.

His doctor collected dolls in national costume.

'I live in fear of withdrawal,' he told the physician. 'My fear of the horrors keeps me drinking.'

He visited Dave in his flat just down the road.

Long-haired and olive-skinned, Dave was a sort of window-cleaning ninja. A Jesusy abseiler. And Dave wore tights which enhanced his incredibly shapely legs.

The guys were talking Herman Hesse and night-blooming cacti when Dave reached into his tights. Probed his tights and plucked out his erection. 'Can you help me with this?' he asked.

DEKA sold capguns and liquorice allsorts, fireworks and methylated spirits.

'I'm painting Our Lady on glass,' the Skull told Joel, 'and I need a load of glittery blue for the robes. Where do I go for glittery blue nail polish?'

*

Joel combed his beard, his chestnut locks. Dressed himself in candy-striped shirt and white tie.

His publisher posed him against a neutral background. Lit him from the side and shot him with a Pentax. (The picture would come out dun and Rembrandtesque, making him look like a rogue probation officer.)

And there in his publisher's loft, he was interviewed by a with-it female journalist. How dark and fair, willowy and buxom, forward and coy and boyish and tender she seemed! Penetratingly lovely, in other words.

She gave him one of her uni-ball pens. Ultramarine.

At the well-attended launch of his slender book of verse, Joel comported himself with tipsy aplomb.

A junior diplomat, an African drummer and a man dressed up as a chicken were among those present.

His publisher kept giving him money. Joel went home to discover crumpled banknotes in all his pockets.

Returning to the venue the following day, he found his unsold books inside the piano.

He woke one morning with a pain in his stomach. A pain between his stomach and his spine.

He felt more than usually faint and sweaty.

When had he last eaten anything? He recalled the flaccid pie of a fortnight ago.

A golden meltdown was taking place in his innards. Important tissues were fuming, dripping goldenly.

He managed to get to his doctor's and lie down on the

floor in the waiting-room.

'Pancreatitis,' said the physician. 'Has it ever struck you that drinking is a low-level search for God?'

With the crystal sludge of pethidine scudding through his veins, Joel lay in hospital and thought stupendous thoughts. Slow-motion thoughts as plumply poised as moons. Colossal thoughts as light as helium.

They've shot me full of sings, Joel thought.

And he dreamed a distant beach he knew did not exist. And here was freedom indeed, the blissful melting away of every inhibition, every smallest worry, and he stripped and was proud of his body, impossibly.

He filmed his movie using an old treadle sewing machine.

Its inky gloss concealed a little hole, an oblong aperture which functioned as a lens.

The antique Singer whirred, ingesting light. Marrying light to brisk, acquisitive emulsions.

A Winter's Tale

When Lambton Quay was redolent of shellfish and brine,
  when Stewart Dawson's corner looked brassy and moist,
    when the cloud above the harbour and the hills was
rich in greys and blues and bluey blacks (a gaseously toxic
spectacle?)—

  at times like these would Liam Mist take mental
photographs, just as if his brain itself consisted of gelatin
and silver halides.

Liam was frowning. The girl in bed beside him had honey-
coloured skin and straight black hair. 'Have you ever had a
nickname?' he asked her.

  'Not to my knowledge,' Lilly Ling replied.

  'I've had a couple, but neither really took.' Liam cleared
his throat. 'Creeping Jesus was one.'

  'Yuck. And the other?'

  'The Pink Panther.'

  Lilly blinked. The girl had smallish breasts with big
black titty nipples. Her pelvis was striped by a skimpy wee
girdle of pale skin, bikini-shaped.

A morning in 197–. The radio was playing 'Haitian Divorce' by Steely Dan. Liam flexed his fingers, then toddled them toward Lilly's nether parts. 'It's penis time again,' he told her sadly. 'It's time alas for another penising.'

'Already? Goodness me.'

Gulls and salty air. Finials and hanging finials. Porches with wine-gum-orange panes, panes of lemon and watery purple.

Liam was long and pale and skinny, but Lilly couldn't get enough of him. In order to put a roof over their heads, she'd sold her violoncello. (The instrument had been a gift from her parents. It travelled in a cello-shaped overcoat.) A single shallow step bisected their room, giving them a kitcheny area and a bedroomy one.

Ants were a problem, yes. This being Oriental Bay, you had to hide the sugar from the ants.

Unheralded and dire, penisings took place with frequency, both at home and abroad. 'I'm breaking my daddy's heart,' gasped Lilly.

On an empty, icy Sunday of stopped clocks and glazed thoroughfares, the dispirited lovers passed the Plaza picture theatre.

Lo, *The Serpent's Egg.*

Liam insisted on sitting right up front, in the first row but one. As the scalloped emerald curtain was about to rise, a mob of ankhed and swastikaed bikies arrived, surrounding Mist and Ling. And though the gangsters drank from many brown bottles, they proved to be a docile, even avid audience.

*

An ankh is a device consisting of a looped bar with a shorter crossbar, used in ancient Egypt as a symbol of life.

Lilly was a proofreader. As she trotted off to work on sandalled feet, her black cape sustained by the haste of her departure, Liam would hope she'd troubled to sponge her cunt.

With the room to himself and the morning before him, he'd *thock* and *thuck* at the solid wee portable he'd salvaged from a skip and mounted atop a tallish chest of drawers, typing up his livid picture-poems.

And when would Liam himself get a job, returning to freight yard or hectic market floor? But when?

Lilly read *Watership Down*. The radio played 'Hey Nineteen' and 'Peg'.

Like a strip of litmus paper, Liam's meaty glans was susceptible to changes of hue. And Lilly liked to finger his mauve or puce helmet, to tease or twink or tweak his glossy knob, sometimes licking the wound of his leaky satin meatus.

The radio played 'Dirty Work'. The radio played 'Babylon Sisters', 'Kid Charlemagne' and 'Deacon Blues'. And Liam Mist conceived . . . of a movie shot at night on the streets of the city, a short but very wet and inky film with no dialogue and a soundtrack by Steely Dan.

Lilly Ling and Liam bloody Mist. From time to time, they'd drop a little speed. Drop a little speed and spot a little hash.

A white white white oblivion with chimes. *Phew* and *What?* and *Holy fucking shit!* Himalayan snows; Patagonian tambourines; Burmese finger cymbals. A sightless bliss of Persil purity.

The French word for pipe is pronounced *peep*. The tygers of wrath are wiser than the horses of instruction.

'We'll get married, Lilly.'

'Yes.'

'We'll queer their pitch by getting married.'

'Yes.'

'Will he like me any better, once I've done the decent?'

'No.'

'Will she?'

'No.'

The southerly flung sleet against the windows. 'So what's for tea, Miss Ling?'

'Duck in orange sauce.'

'Duck in orange sauce?'

'It comes in a grubby tin with a dragon on. I also bought some incense and long-grained rice.'

'Good for you.'

When the power failed, Lilly lit a candle.

Apex Landscaping

i) Barrett and Kiszco were digging a hole. Barrett dropped his shovel and went for his tape measure. 'Hold this end, you fool. I want to get an idea.'

Said Kiszco, 'I've got a couple you can have.'

'An idea of how we're getting on. Of how much of this mother we've yet to dig.'

Measuring. More digging.

'How come you never get any sex, Barrett?'

'I never hit on anyone, and no one ever hits on me. It's a Law of Nature.'

Kiszco was Barrett's labourer. Shaven head, rings through the eyebrows, boots with scores of eyelets and metres of lace.

ii) Already the hole was huge, a vast excavation. Sometimes Kiszco pissed in it. And Kiszco wrote songs, one of which he dedicated to his employer.

'Oh where has it gone my life
But down the friggin' pan?
Of what has my life consisted
But bread and marmalade jam?

'Oh where has it gone my life
But down the friggin' pan?
Of what has it consisted
But lettuce and cold ham?'

These were the words Kiszco sang to Barrett, strumming his rattly guitar in the smoko shed. 'Do you like it?' he paused to ask.

'It's absolute shite,' said Barrett. 'It's a truly, awfully, deeply terrible song.'

'Hey but dude,' said Kiszco, '*this is your own tiresome plaint* I'm iterating here.'

iii) 'There *was* a woman,' said Barrett. 'I sent her certain letters. I wrote to her professing certain sentiments.'

'Fatal, man. A *big* mistake,' said Kiszco.

'She didn't want my letters, nor yet my moony, heartfelt sentiments.'

'Predictably enough. Predictably enough.'

'Do we know what they *do* want, women?'

'Do we hell,' said Kiszco. 'I'll swap you a sardine for a peanut-butter.'

iv) Kiszco and Kate were entertaining Betty. Kiszco and Kate and Betty had smoked a little shit and drunk a little ouzo.

The flat had matt-black walls, articulated lamps like giant grasshoppers. There was also a coffee table with books and magazines: *Four Quartets, Rolling Stone, Flowers for Hitler, American Rifleman.*

Barrett arrived bearing chocolates and wine. He was sporting a ten-cent tie with Eiffel Towers. 'Hi. Apologies. Public transport's a wonderful thing, until you have to use it.'

'I've heard so much about you,' Betty said.

'Really?'

'Perhaps not. I'm given to exaggeration.'

v) Dinner was served: spaghetti Bolognese. Brought to the table in a crock, Kiszco's sauce suggested a cloacal sort of lava.

Betty seemed to have quite an appetite. 'So you're Kiszco's boss?'

'That's right,' said Barrett.

'And what do you two *do* all day?'

'We dig bloody holes. And then we fill them in.'

'?'

'We're Apex Landscaping. We're godless improvers of the Earth's unsightly bits.'

Said Betty, 'I myself paint forceful wee abstracts.'

vi) Barrett waited for three days before ringing Betty. (A lot can happen in three days, but not much happened to Barrett.

The smoko shed. Kiszco. 'Have you ever noticed that when we move on to a section and begin to carve her up with our picks and shovels, it isn't long before all the birds clear off?'

'I have indeed,' said Barrett.

'It's like we sort of poison and pollute.'

'It is. Lamentably.'

A pause. Presently, Kiszco broke the silence. 'Shall I sing you my latest song?'

'Shit no. No need for that *at all!*')

vii) Barrett took Betty to the Winter Show. The would-be lovers went for a ride on the Ghost Train, enjoying its corny thrills. They watched a Chinese magician (naked to the waist) snatch from his armpit a laden goldfish bowl.

'Seldom have I seen such a yummy physique,' said Betty.

Hot dogs. Candyfloss. Rising through the night in the Ferris wheel's chill gondola, Barrett and Betty were grateful for one another's warmth.

Barrett gave Betty's mittened hand a squeeze. 'We're all in recovery from having been children,' he told her. 'We must learn to desire with guile and without hope.'

viii) Barrett received a letter from Jones of Zenith Drains.

Dear B.,

Can I interest you in a small mechanical digger of purple and green? Come and take a look and make me an offer. Fact is, I'm off to Nebraska, the 'cornhusker' state. It's the home of the Western meadow lark. Ditto the cottonwood and the goldenrod (a tree and a flower, respectively).

Cheers etc., Taffy

ix) Betty took Barrett to a movie. The girl vending popcorn was wearing a T-shirt that read AND THUS I CLOTHE MY NAKED VILLAINY.

The film was the work of a celebrated Indian master. The women of a dusty Indian village ... were being terrorised by something or someone. A rapist? A tiger? Barrett couldn't decide. It was far and away the worst movie he had ever seen, in every respect.

Said Betty, 'I'd like you to take me to your place and bonk me silly.'

'I'm not surprised,' said Barrett.

x) A taxi ride. A scramble. Barrett unlocking a door and lighting a candle.

'So let me get this straight,' Betty said. *'You're living in this hut we're standing in?'*

'More or less.'

Betty surveyed the clutter of picks and shovels and

wheelbarrows in Barrett's smoko shed. Beneath a mechanical digger of purple and green, Barrett had installed a mattress and an alarm clock. 'But how do you *cook?*' the lady wanted to know.

'I eat out a lot,' Barrett conceded.

'I'm shocked,' said Betty, 'that you should bring me here.'

'I don't know what came over me. Can I take it that that *fuck* is out of the question now?'

xi) With freshly shaven head and new tattoo, Kiszco took advantage of the open mike at a blues club to make his début as a singer and songsmith.

Barrett had drunk thirteen tequilas. 'Break a neck,' he said as Kiszco rose to perform.

'Oh hear me comin' baby,
My love's a big choo-choo,
I'm aimin' down the tracks a mile
To couple nice with you.

'Oh hear me comin' baby,
My heart's a big freight train,
I'm figurin' you're hot to pop
My whistle once again.'

This was the song Kiszco sang to the folks at the Blue Mushroom. Barrett sculled tequilas fourteen, fifteen and sixteen . . . *in rapid succession.*

xii) No more Betty, no. But Barrett was the lucky and sentimental owner of *one* of her forceful wee abstracts (oil on board). He hung it in the gloom of the smoko shed, where it blazed like a single lambent sunflower.

The purple-and-green digger proved to have been a canny investment. It could brew a pot of tea and iron shirts, and it ate its baked beans nicely, using chopsticks.

A single lambent sunflower.

Down Through the Pines

CHAPTER 1

A postcard from a friend visiting Cedar Rapids, Ohio. It shows Einstein at the beach, a beach somewhere. And Einstein looks exactly like Einstein, Albert, physicist and Nobel laureate, but is wearing shorts and sandals. The Einstein face is graced by an expression of mildly amused braininess or pleasant imbecility, take your pick. The Einstein shorts are unremarkable, not particularly dated to look at, and the legs are OK legs, not too bad at all if somewhat hairless, but oh my God the sandals. They seem to have something of a *heel*; the peekaboo toes consist of dome-shaped apertures, vents like Turkish domes in silhouette. Onion domes or twirly confectioner's kisses.

Yes: the Einstein sandals of 1945 . . . *are almost certainly a woman's.*

CHAPTER 2

My friend the postman has travelled to the four corners of the world. Travels every year on his meagre postman's pay to some fresh destination, there to revel in fresh discomforts and inconveniences.

I leave the travelling to others. I stay at home and read and watch a bit of telly. When one's own habitation provides a sufficiency of annoyances, why go abroad? Letterbox and telephone furnish all the alarms I can cope with.

My name is Bruno Swan. Some sixteen years ago, I was coming to an end. The lights were going out all over Bruno. Today, I live a posthumous sort of life, one nonetheless replete with quiet satisfactions.

CHAPTER 3

My friend the postman is beginning to limp like a knackered dromedary. 'Seen anything decent recently?' I ask him.

'I haven't been to a film in months,' says Martin.

'No? My late father used to boast that he'd seen every movie made before the end of World War II.'

'Quite. Some people simply swear off the cinema. Give it up, like smoking.'

'They do. But retreat perhaps to the reeking wasteland of television.'

As well as being a traveller, Martin's an omnivorous reader. His long brown face is handsomely lined, and has about it something of sage Arabian dignity, the wisdom of the oasis. 'Television? I'll tell you who likes television,' the weathered Bedouin says.

'Who?'

'Poor old Johnny Bray. Poor old Johnny Bray has taken to knocking on my door from time to time.'

'Ah.'

'It's late in the afternoon and there he is. Can he come in and play the piano? Can he come in and watch *Spongebob Squarepants*?'

'He's apologetic, but.'

'He laughs so much it's almost a delight. He laughs so hard at Spongebob fucking Squarepants, it's almost a pleasure to have him in the house.'

CHAPTER 4

Neil Young has a heartbreaking voice. Neil Young has a heartbreaking voice.

Somewhere back in the 80s, I stood in a bottle store and watched a video clip of Young performing 'Like a Hurricane'. There he was on the screen above my head, singing and strumming while being blustered silly, stormily mauled by a wind machine, *I wanna love you but I'm getting blown away* . . .

The guitar work on 'Hurricane' is astral, titanic. Time and time again, I sit in the dark and let it do its thing, sit in the dark and let it take me apart.

CHAPTER 5

I'm stopped in the street by a bronzed, a blond young man. Levis, T-shirt, designer stubble. 'What's that over there?' he asks.

His accent is English. 'It used to be a museum,' I tell him, 'and to the left you've got your carillon and war memorial.'

'Cool,' he says. 'Thank you.'

I walk along Arthur to the top of Cuba. On the corner

is the house in which I spent the first few months of my sobriety, living above an empty shop.

It remains a sooty, dim, Dickensian address. Soon to be stomped by the new, obliterating motorway. In a bedroom at the rear, I finished writing *Tartan Revolver*, the first of my three published books. I'd bought for the purpose a fat little manual in two tones of grey; when you pushed the plump red lozenge of a certain mysterious key, its carriage would track from right to left with an oily sort of thrum: *yoddle-oddle-oddle-oddle-oddle.*

Behind that window up there, I completed a vivid, skinny novel, yes. And it might be fun to get a picture, take a photo of those doomed, disappointed-seeming panes. A Fujicolor disposable would do the trick, but I'd have lots of film left over.

CHAPTER 6

My present address is temporary. No sleek savvy cat dozes on the fire escape, nor are my neighbours prostitutes and members of Black Power, but I like and use the peace and quiet here. If I duck down through the pines to Wallace Street, I can be in the city in twenty minutes.

I keep the joint uncluttered, low on visual noise. The spines of a hundred books and a Chinese wall-hanging—I confess to finding colour enough in these.

CHAPTER 7

With regard to my worthless Chinese banderole: in search perhaps of balance, centredness, I sometimes contemplate its ghostly torrents, its floaty crags.

The Chinese seem to manage not to rear psychopathic monsters. The Chinese are sane and nicely made (I've noticed that the young men tend to have good legs).

The truth of the matter is, I like the Chinese. I like their restaurants and cafés; I like their tanks of goldfish, their glossy black enamel, their lanterns with scarlet tassels. I like the sweet and sour of their temperate, amusable demeanours.

As the coal-burning city steams its way toward nightfall, I picture myself living in some muggy Chinatown, renting a room above a busy kitchen, playing noughts and crosses on a grimy little board of teak and porcelain. Smoking my opium.

'You wouldn't like it,' says Martin. (A dollop of clarification: my friend the postman is not of course *my* postman. We meet in town, if we meet at all, only when he's completed his route and is making his way home.)

'You're right,' I say. 'Forget the opium.'

'I'm not depriving you of your narcotic. It's just that you'd find the Chinese world too populous and hectic.'

'Probably. What with all that gambling, all those tong vendettas.'

'Quite. So what are you reading, at the moment?'

'Don DeLillo's *Underworld*. For the fourth time. *Underworld* is the book for me.'

'The one you take to the desert island?'

'Absolutely. There are more stories in *Underworld* . . . than are actually *in Underworld*. DeLillo's *Underworld* . . . extends to infinity in all directions.'

CHAPTER 8

I seem to be forever buying milk. Buying milk or thinking that the blood-vessels in my right leg are collapsing. And yet I've had my picture in the paper, been on the radio.

CHAPTER 9

My dream goes something like this:

Good Friday in a detox ward somewhere. The sweet, metallic smell of Wattie's canned spaghetti.

A pathetically sweaty Greek gangster has the bed next to mine. 'I'm shaking like a jelly over here.'

'Just hang tough,' I tell him.

'When's our next medication due?'

'God knows.'

'I can feel some kind of seizure coming on. I've wrought some fucking havoc in me time, but I don't deserve this.'

'What goes up must come down. Or something.'

'Them Nazis out the nursing station—the filph is *toffs* compared!'

My dead but ageless father appears. Suit and tie, hair parted wetly, familiar gold ring. 'I've always liked this town. Denny Mahon and I were stationed here during the early part of the war. I thought I'd take the bus out to the old aerodrome, have a look around.'

'Do that, Dad.'

'Will I see you at all, you know, when you grow up? Will there be a number I can ring?'

Dr Mephisto is next. Earring, three days' growth, soap-scented hands. (What do they want with me, these attractive young men?) 'Your pancreas is inflamed. Likewise your already fatty liver.'

'No kidding.'

'Ever had a shot of benzoethylcryptotriplicate?'

'No.'

'Hurts like hell, believe me. What are your thoughts on Dreiser?'

'I've never read him. The last ten minutes of *Carrie* were terrific.'

'You're referring to the William Wyler film?'

'With Laurence Olivier, yes. With Laurence Olivier being utterly tragic.'

'I put it to you that Don DeLillo is *not* the totally groovy, funky and together, hip wizard seer you think he is.'

'He's merely very good. Is what I think.'

'Don DeLillo sucks. Ditto Bruno Swan and *Tartan Revolver*. I'm tempted to reach for the hurty stuff.'

Sacraments

1

The city has Finnish-looking trams. Ferries, helicopters and Finnish-looking trams.

A tennis court stands next to a cathedral. A sandwich bar embarrasses a Theosophical temple.

Some of the smaller banks have tinted windows, science-fiction panes the colour of petrol. And the Yohst and Kubrick Centre in Bilton Square wears copper epaulettes; at night, it's painted by floodlights of lime and guava-pink.

As three a.m. approaches, the station settles down, achieves a degree of equilibrium. It loosens its belt (as it were) and breathes a little easier. And the mad and the bad and the sad in the cells downstairs? They admit defeat and shut up—finally.

Detective Mark Traven rises from his desk. Time to empty the bladder and stretch the legs. In white shirt and loud floral tie, Mark looks like a shoulder-holstered Mormon, trim and youthful and smoothly truculent.

He drifts toward Stella Greybill's desk. She's up to her

armpits in files, her messy hair a storm of golden wisps. 'Cut your crap, Traven.'

'I haven't said a word.'

'This place stinks of fries and hamburgers.'

'Yours and mine,' says Mark, 'but mostly mine.'

'Ain't that the truth.'

'We should be the subject of a study. The scientists should study us long and hard. Nutritionists with clipboards, probing the mysteries of our bright eyes and bushy tails.'

'Grow fucking up.' Is what Stella says.

'I'm closing fast on my next cigarette. I'm cruising stealthily.'

'Not me. Not *this* detective. What *I* want is beef tea, if you're passing the machine.'

'Beef tea? Since when? These are questions the machine itself will ask.'

'The secret is not to bully it. The secret is to let it do its thing.'

2

The convent is that of the Sisters of Abiding Comfort, a dwindling community of tough, cheerful souls. The nuns have their business in the city, with the desperate, but their home stands on the side of a bushy vale in a quiet eastern suburb.

Convent and playfully Gothic chapel: few people know of their existence. A circumstance that Robert Sharland does his best to perpetuate.

He's here again this morning, in the first pew but one. He likes the altar of white marble, the lilies and the candlesticks of blond brass. Enjoys the windows and the watery stains they impart, palest tincturings of lemon and rose. His bodyguard is armed and wired for sound and sits one row behind his principal, apparently unfazed by the dour Latin mass.

Bread and wine are at hand. Chalice and ciborium. The sacrament achieves its overcast plateau, and the priest says the occult words of consecration. How does Matthew have it? '"This is my body. But behold the hand of him who betrays me is with me on the table."' Something like that, Sharland thinks. And Matthew's is a painterly effect, with candlelight and gloom interpenetrating.

The nuns like Sharland to breakfast at the convent. Swap pleasantries with the visiting celebrant.

Two places have been set at one end of a long table. The room itself (a small refectory?) has plastered walls, a floor of reddish tiles. Sharland's bodyguard seats his employer, places a cellphone beside Robert's plate and retires to a chair just inside the door.

Stripped of his vestments now, dog-collared Father Conway makes his appearance. 'It's toast and jam and boiled eggs, I see. The sisters seem to want to feed us up.'

'Good morning, Father.'

The smiley little priest's as plump as a sparrow. And layman and cleric are by no means strangers. 'You turned in a brisk performance this morning.'

'Did I now,' says Conway. 'Perhaps I'd counted the house.'

'You'll have noticed that I never take Communion.'

'I've noticed that your minder sometimes does.'

'I'm a product of my education, Vince. I believe in the mass without believing.'

'Surely not.'

'I believe in the mass. Without believing.'

'Well I wonder now how that can be. I do.'

A nun arrives with more triangles of toast. Orange juice in a stainless-steel jug. 'Shall I do you another egg, Father?'

'I think not, Sister Joan, on this occasion.'

Sharland waits until the nun has gone. Resumes his 'confession' in a somewhat cooler tone. 'I'm a powerful man, Vincent. I make things happen. My puissance flows out into the world to sink and saturate, penetrating systems from top to bottom.'

'Oh?'

'I trickle down. Through structures, institutions. I might be likened to the Holy Ghost.'

'Hubris. Blasphemy. To say nothing of the lesser sin of rank hyperbole.'

'I export and import and rake in dividends. Power begets wealth and wealth begets power. But among my hobbies is dealing in pictures. It's well within my competence to anoint struggling artists, and this it amuses me to do. I make their reputations and begin to sell their paintings for surprising new sums. I feather their nests while also upholstering my own. Does this make me virtuous, or am I merely acting out of self-interest?'

'Both. You're having a bob each way, like most of the rest of us.'

Robert's cellphone trills. He picks it up and jabs one of its buttons. 'You've reached Sharland. Speak.'

The bodyguard approaches and addresses Conway.

38

'The Rolls will soon be brought to the side door, Father. Can we offer you a lift anywhere?'

'That's thoughful of you, Taube.'

'Sell sell sell,' says Sharland. Talking of course to his coal-black Nokia.

3

It's Tuesday morning, and this is Eric Jones. He's sporting the maroon thumbnail, the big black shapely fuck-you Druid's hood. Yes, hooded is exactly how he likes to feel.

For a period of time. For a period of time, he stands in the doorway of a camera shop and watches the mall. But then a blue midmorning whim flares like a match in him. Prompts him to stir and straighten up, muster and marshal forces.

Bamboo Grove Apartments are tricky to get into. You have to wait for a citizen to exit, then duck inside with no apologies. On the third shallow floor lives Henry Hawke, the oldest surviving junkie in the realm, notorious and grey.

Notorious and grey and pigeon-chested. Like some derelict knight of yore, bony and big-knuckled. 'Look what washes up. Just as I'm about to have my lunch.'

'Lunch? You?'

'I pick. I pick.'

'I'm Eric if you've forgotten.'

'Yes. No. I remember you from that Narcotics Anonymous meeting. So how's the battle, Eric?'

'I slipped. I crashed and burned.'

'So what the fuck is new? But never mind. Would you like a cup of coffee?'

The man himself, at home. A steely cook and chemist of the old school, ground and sanded to a narrow-shouldered skeleton, a bristly skull with Auschwitz-ashen temples, skin as grey as dishwater. 'The name of Henry Hawke has entered the textbooks. I've outlived any number of quacks, addiction specialists and hepatologists. To say nothing of cops and probies.'

'Hepatologists.'

'I buried my own lovely brother. Also several arseholes of whom I was fond. But Craig lies in a quiet place, and I know I could have taken better care of him.'

'Yeah?'

'Yeah. And how are you having this coffee of yours?'

A Buddha here, a crucifix there. Many antique LPs are angle-parked along the skirting-board. The silent Panasonic is tuned to the horse-racing channel, its screen a brilliantly colourful display.

Henry lives on Nicorette gum, with hogget and tepid gravy delivered by Meals on Wheels. And Eric Jones observes him, and not without respect. 'I graduated from smack to methadone. I got my shit together,' Henry continues, 'and even began to drink. Imagine it. I took to the grog and thought I'd joined the human race. Methadone and Mogadon and wine. With taxis to the pharmacy, the bottle store. Plus also I smoked to the level of national representative.'

'Carbon monoxide. Tars.'

'Where are you stopping now?'

'Here and there. I'm seeing a chick.'

40

'And you're keeping your hand in, I suppose.'

'Xylox. I'm moving a little xylox.'

'What can I tell you? You've got to get back on the horse, begin again. You should at least continue with the meetings.'

'I could maybe handle a treatment centre. When I'm good and ready, like.'

'Shrinks and cardiologists and kidney guys—they all despaired of me. Said I was in for death or insanity.'

'They love that line.'

'Years passed. Decades. And then one day I couldn't do it anymore. I was sick of the hideous weight, the unabating demands of my addictions. I was sick and tired of the huge responsibility of being me.'

As a maker of instant coffee, Henry is not deficient in technique: the milky brew he hands to his guest at last is free from undissolved clots of powder. 'I need a lucky break,' Eric ventures.

'You need a lucky break, which is what I got. It was as if a clock had wound itself down and finally stopped ticking. Some sort of inner, organic clock, the thing that had craved and hungered through thousands of days and nights. Silent now, defunct.'

'This gives me hope. No shit.'

'My very own brother lies in a quiet place.' Henry indicates a framed photograph. 'The pair of us at the races. Seventy-six, that was. I guess you can tell by the Starsky and Hutch costumes.'

'Disco lives.'

'And what about yourself? Do you have any brothers anywhere?'

Eric shrugs. Sips at his coffee and makes a face. 'Christ. Point me at that sugar bowl, Henry.'

4

The city grows ever more concrete. The city grows ever more abstract and abstruse.

He smokes a little weed, shifts a little xylox. And Eric has his hood deployed again; the modelled, Druidical cowl seals and finishes him.

Wednesday afternoon. A whitish glare replaces shadows, contrasts. This is the whiteness of X-rays and photographic negatives.

He's in a mothish mood to maybe go again, trouble the flame a second time, for Henry Hawke has something Eric needs. Not that Eric can put his finger on it. Not that he can know quite what he's in for.

Henry's front door has been left ajar.

Eric knocks on the jamb—with no result. Calls out Henry's name—to no effect. But Eric was born to push and probe, to test the elasticity of boundaries and borders, to ease himself forward with pre-emptive stealth.

The beautiful telly thrives, a colour-oven. Old Spice talcum powder scents the air, and a towel lies on the carpet near Henry's ivory foot. Henry himself is wearing a khaki bathrobe. He has obviously showered and clipped his toenails, and now he's resting up. Is sitting on a chair at one end of his Formica table, his back to the wall and his softened eyes in neutral.

And he could indeed be watching *Charlie's* fucking

Angels—except that he's plainly far too dead to be watching anything.

This is Eric's first dead body. Seated as if relaxed, its left arm supported by the table, it seems a thing of touching poise and lightness. And Eric is not afraid to bend, incline his ear to the slightly parted lips, glance into the clement, disconnected peepers.

No breath, no sounds of breathing. No pulse in carotid, jugular. And Henry Hawke's grey cheek feels less than living, even less than fleshy. No point really in attempting mouth-to-mouth; no point either, much, in ringing for an ambulance. Also, and of maximum importance: the person reporting coming across the corpse is always of interest to the cops. Becomes in fact a popular interviewee, where foul play is suspected. But Eric can detect zero signs of violence.

Best to do the bizzo and clear off. Best to take what's up for grabs and fuck off out of it.

He swishes the $375 he finds in Henry's wallet, but what else is of value? Henry's vintage LPs are useless to Eric. Even if he knew what he was dealing with (Iron Butterfly, Jefferson Airplane and Tangerine Dream, for instance), he has no means of playing them. And then he discovers the. And then he discovers oh Jesus yes the gun. He opens a kitchen drawer and there it is, in the roomy part behind the wells for knives and forks: a bluish, satin-finished .38 that fits and fills his hand, making him feel both smart and ballsy as.

CONFIDENTIAL TRANSCRIPT

Laszlo Sinclair is twenty-three and works as a theatrical electrician. He was the subject of surveillance from June to September of this year. A number of charges have been laid (see attachment).

DETECTIVE STELLA GREYBILL: I'm sitting here. I'm waiting.

LASZLO SINCLAIR: (Inaudible.)

GREYBILL: Fill me in, Laszlo. Illuminate this mess.

SINCLAIR: (Inaudible.)

GREYBILL: You don't think you can? So make like a thing with a spine and give it a shot.

SINCLAIR: Xylox is very kind to one at first, but it soon becomes this total preoccupation.

GREYBILL: Now *there's* a surprise.

SINCLAIR: I went to Larsen's Crossing in the early hours of Sunday morning. I'd swallowed a tab at final curtain, and I went to Larsen's Crossing with a member of the cast. And in this actor's shitty little flat, with a neon sign for beer just outside the window, I saw the gods.

GREYBILL: You saw the what?

SINCLAIR: Ken plays Mungo in *Walking Tall*. We'd gone to a neighbourhood bar, slurped some suds and walked back to his place. Thunder and a deluge just as we got in.

GREYBILL: And?

SINCLAIR: Kenneth crashes out, goodbye and thanks a lot. Just me and the cat and the beer sign after that.

GREYBILL: Just you and the cat. Go on.

SINCLAIR: I look at my watch and it's four o'clock. When I look again, it's ten minutes earlier, the second hand's adopted an anticlockwise sweep, and it's welcome to psychosis Lasz you sorry fuck.

GREYBILL: Xylox. The *good* shit, right? A Day-Glo-orange tablet with a wee X on it.

SINCLAIR: The beer sign stops flashing and the cat stops breathing. And I myself am dead, stopped and null like a disused abattoir. And then I see the gods in their hundreds, the brown gods in their thousands. Tier upon tier of them, back and back to infinity, a sort of tessellation of sage brown faces.

GREYBILL: (Inaudible.)

SINCLAIR: Sage brown faces, back and back and back.

Tattoo

Marcus was released from the clinic on a grey, humid, drizzly day in April.

By five o'clock that evening, he'd found a suitable flat. The block itself was situated in a sodden little gully of a street.

Behold a tiny kitchen like the galley on a trawler, its stinky black stove petite and personable! Marcus was also beguiled by the rest of the mouldy dump—he'd long aspired to living in just such a windowless bunker: a womb with*out* a view.

'It could do with an airing,' said the woman.

'Who the hell are you?'

'I'm Mrs Sykes. From the floor above.'

'Goodbye, Mrs Sykes.'

Marcus wore his wheat-coloured coat in the Continental manner, leaving the sleeves empty. When the Salvation Army van arrived, he directed operations like a caped gendarme, disposing the junk he'd bought earlier in the day. Mattress, blankets, small cuboidal fridge: these and an armchair were all his possessions now. Well, almost.

He opened his only suitcase. Sandwiched between two of his best shirts, the tastefully gilt-framed oil was small and square; Marcus took the painting from the case and stood it on the seat of the armchair.

'Shall I fetch you down a cuppa?' the Sykes woman asked.

'No. Enough already.'

'You can tell me to mind my own business, but you shouldn't wear jeans with a nice coat like that.'

'Should I not?'

'It's a *great* mistake, in my opinion. What's your line of work, if you don't mind my asking?'

'Demolition. Boom.'

'I don't know how to take you, I'm sure I don't.'

Marcus lifted a bottle from his suitcase. The poison of his choice was Tattoo, a vodka-and-cranberry cocktail with a red-and-green dragon on the label. Bold, romantic, maritime Marcus!—he swigged a mighty swig of dragons and tattoos, toasting distant Shanghai mentally.

'I don't think much of that painting,' the Sykes person announced.

'You really must stop barging in like this.'

'A country road with bits of snow and mud. There's not much to it, is there?'

'Not much at all. Deliciously.'

'Would I know the artist?'

'I shouldn't think so. His name was Maurice Vlaminck.'

'?'

'A motor mechanic by trade, he played the violin in the gypsy orchestras of Montmartre.'

'!'

'Derain gives him a pipe. A painter and a poet, was Vlaminck. Billiards he liked, and tennis—and wrestling and cycling and driving racing cars.'

'You seem to know an awful lot about him.'

'In 1945, he published a book called *Radios Clandestins*.'

'So what are you really? A writer?'

'No no no, Mrs Sykes. My name is Marcus Darke and I'm an actor.'

'Like Peter O'Toole and Al Pacino?'

'Like Peter O'Toole and Al Pacino, yes.'

'But have I ever seen you on the telly?'

'I prefer to work on the stage.'

'Mind what you're doing with that bottle! You're slopping your dripper, Mr Darke.'

'So I am. How careless of me. Would you like a snort yourself?'

'I think not, under the circumstances.'

Marcus considered the cold lights in his bottle. 'I prefer to work on the stage, but I don't get the parts anymore. I'm *rest*ing, Mrs Sykes, and I have been for some time. I've been resting, yes, for years, and now I'm slopping my dripper, and soon I'm going to throw you out and take my medication.'

'Medication, Mr Darke?'

'"I could be bounded in a nutshell, and count myself a king of infinite space, were it not that I have bad dreams."'

'*Night*mares, Mr Darke?'

'But not just at night, Mrs Sykes.'

2

BRINDLE EMBERS

. . . I would like those who think of themselves as disciples of the flame not to lose sight of the tranquil, arduous lesson of the crystal.
Italo Calvino

BRINDLE EMBERS

Down and Saffron

She didn't like him much, nor Sis didn't care for him neither, and what could you do but give him the cold shoulder? Adding a bit of strong to his cup of tea, passing a plate of scones or what have you, she showed him as much coolness as she dared.

If Grace sometimes smiled at her own stubbornness, Sis would never relent. 'He picks his teeth,' said she, '—not that there's many left to pick.'

He wasn't *ancient*, mind. When he came to their feminine board, he brought dainty presents for Ma, coloured soaps and scented French waters. His high collar seemed to bite into his neck. A buyer and seller of livestock, he had an indoors pallor and favoured carmine neckties. You wouldn't mind him for a distant cousin, but not as a stepfather.

'If he comes at Christmas,' said Sis, 'we'll know it's serious.'

Ma remained tight-lipped, given to a solemn introspection. Attempting to forget her late husband, she forgot her daughters too. And Mother was prey to fits of stillness, her sudsy wrists suspended above the copper. Coming to, she'd fret. 'With my hands all chafed and red, what man will have me, Grace?'

Beside the meat safe hung an Advent calendar. Each morning when the cow had been milked and the new-lain eggs fetched in, Sis opened a papery window. Drummer boys and snowmen, chimney sweeps and magi appeared, a fresh revelation every day.

And soon the holy event was upon them. Mother and daughters trudged through scraps of snow to midnight mass in the village. And Mister Dignan in his carmine tie whisked them home in a trap, coming inside for whiskey and a slice of Christmas cake. He had something for Mother, of course: a parcel of linen all the way from Dublin. What could you do but answer when spoken to, pass the cruet of toothpicks to his end of the table?

Early in the year of 1884, on Grace's twelfth birthday, Ma announced her engagement to Mister Dignan. Her tone was doubtful—awed but sceptical.

'And when will you wed, Mother?' Gracie asked.

'When Mister Dignan settles, I imagine.'

Now, the county of Eire was all very well for some. But Grace, the elder daughter and spit of her dark-eyed mother, had begun to long for warmth and bloody sunsets. She'd read about the yellow rose of Texas, the blue grass of Kentucky; she even fancied her chances in the fecund canyons of New York City. Lying abed with her sister, aware of the gentle rain licking the stones in the yard, it was as if she questioned the darkness. 'Shall you come with me to America, Sis?'

'But I'm only eight, Gracie.'

'We'll study elocution. We don't want people thinking we're greenhorns.'

'What's a greenhorn, pray?'

Dublin was noted for its biscuits and stout. In Phoenix Park there dwelt exotic animals. At the wharves of Dublin or Dun Laoghaire, Grace would find a ship. Bedazzled, passionate, she pictured the tall three-master. To ride the sixteen mile on Connor's dray would cost nothing. And if you ignored the need for money, holding fast to pluck, determination . . . The girls broke open their piggy banks, nonetheless.

The appointed morning came. The sky was livid, the paddock a mire.

'We're going to town for the day,' Gracie whispered. Connor seemed unmoved. 'It's no business of mine. Just don't be seen.'

When the carter pushed Sis up onto the dray, Grace drew her down between the bales. And pity for Ma was somehow smothered—in naughtiness, resolve, dislike of Mister Dignan.

The sisters sang for coins on a Dublin pavement. An ostler bade them sleep in a loft above a stable. To a Jewish silversmith with silver in his teeth, Grace sold her brooch, the 'heirloom' her granny had bequeathed her, never to see it again and good riddance. At the end of an enterprising week, the girls went to the harbour hand in hand. And there amid the spars and figureheads they gave a sailor their money and were soon aboard a ship.

The handsome tar had pointy black whiskers. 'And where would you like to be put off?'

'Our hearts are set on America,' said Sis.

'We'd settle for New York,' Grace allowed.

The tar winked mightily. 'When I speak to the Old Man next, I'll make particular mention.'

Below decks, a salt and heaving gloom, bowls of tepid swill and vomiting. There in the sloshing bin of steerage, Grace began to menstruate. And in the shadows, and not always at night, the pizzles of the dour husbands jutted.

'The rain in Spain stays mainly on the plain.' Though Grace tried to modify her speech, the down and saffron of her lilt persisted. If she spoke like a goombah, so be it: she'd throw her little book into the wash.

The sea was blue but the vessel's wake was green. That happy circumstance seemed to bode well for the sisters. But when at last the ship dropped anchor, Grace was to hear unpleasant news. As she stood at the rail with Sis beside her, it wasn't Manhattan's skyline she beheld, nor yet the spiky aura of some titanic statue. What lay before her was the harbour at Bluff, New Zealand. And when the cook had told her where they were, explaining their incredible location, her grievous disappointment struck her dumb.

Working with Coppola

1976. The Philippines. We're engaged in a muddy mock war, grotesque simulacrum of the real thing.

Plastic apocalypse. Violin spiders. The drenching monsoon slicks our ponchos and tarpaulins. We've got helicopters, crates of M-16s, smokes in all the colours of the Max Factor range. There's no shortage of Purple Haze and Clear Light, either.

I may be only a lousy dialogue coach (whatever one of *those* is), but Eleanor Coppola confides in me. 'We're eating mangoes and swatting mosquitoes. This is the moment I've dreamed of being present at. Francis is revealed as the conceptual artist I've been longing to know.'

The director himself takes a different view. 'This is *crazy* shit. We're in the jungle, we've access to too much money and too much equipment, and little by fucking little we're going insane!'

Our most important set is wrecked by a typhoon. Martin Sheen has a heart attack and his brother is hired to stand in for him. We're shooting a key battle sequence (a complex aerial ballet) when the government choppers on loan to us are called away abruptly. And when in the fullness of time Brando arrives, he proves to be overweight and underprepared. 'How can he let me *down* like this?' Francis anguishes. .

'He's too fat to play Kurtz?' I ask.

'Kurtz is supposed to look . . . *like Kurtz is supposed to look.*'

'Like *tall*?' I suggest.

'Tall we can do. We'll shoot Pete Cooper from behind. We'll use Pete Cooper as Marlon's body double. Perhaps you can teach him that bumpy grindy thing Marlon does with his hip.'

'Bumpy grindy thing?'

'And see what you can do to get Marlon reading. I want him steeped in Conrad's sombre prose.'

And thus it comes to pass that I school the great actor in *Heart of Darkness*. ('"Going up that river was like travelling back to the earliest beginnings of the world, when vegetation rioted on tile earth and the big trees were kings."') We sit at a table outdoors, Brando savours a local risotto, a helium moon of lipstick pink ascends, those violin spiders are everywhere gestating—and I am gravid with the sick suspicion that

Sin City

The Yanks were still in Vietnam, killing and being killed. On the streets of Wellington, Ashley Gibb was feeling the need for warmer clothing. Winter had come and he'd donned a pullover. A Nehru shirt and a tatty grey jumper— that was his whack.

Though he didn't quite see her as being a woman, Rebecca was the *girl* he'd always wanted. She wore blouses of a spooky Persil whiteness. She filled her jeans nicely, was careful about the freshness of her tops. And her blue eyes were moist and healthy looking; they photographed you through a coating of bright fluid.

Dalton had position, clothes, a troubled wife. Never quite at home among the hippies, the older guy had scored this gorgeous hippy chick. 'We're drinking in the other bar, Ashley. Perhaps you'd like to join us.'

It was all the same to Ash. His thoughts were governed by the smug conviction that *he* could never succeed with Rebecca. When she saw him approaching she seemed to darken, slump into deflation and disgust. It was almost a blush, this murky frown of hers, this swampy look of skirmish and bloodshed. 'Not you again, you jerk.'

'Dalton asked me over.'

'And you had to *come*, of course. You're a fucking ningnong, Gibb.'

She used an oil or lotion, the scent of which reminded Ash of fennel. Her face was somewhat gaunt, her long cheek a lilac-tinted shadow. And her cheekbones were high and prominent, seeming to lift her face toward you with a tilt, an upward proffering. But though he saw her clearly enough (as if through that enhancing film which bathed her own quick eye), Ash didn't stand a chance, he hadn't got a bolter's.

College had ended badly. College had ended in failure and shame. He'd already put a couple of jobs behind him (cleaning windows, humping freight), placements in which he'd been of no more use than the next bloke. At present he was living on his wits—cadging, making do. He trudged the wet pavements, read novels in the New Zealand Room. Sometimes he craved a pie, a crumbed sausage, a fried egg. More often than not, he craved alcohol.

Where did he sleep? It was anything but clear, even to himself. From day to day, a new place emerged as a likely destination for the night ahead. A couch would do, a floor.

In certain lights, the city looked tenebrous, bat-ridden. On cornices and ledges and the tongues of mild gargoyles, Dickensian soot accumulated. And a single grotty pub was where it was at. Its carpets were sodden, sticky with filth.

On this particular evening, a cold southerly was keeping folk at home. Ashley, broke, was standing at a leaner. Out of his line of sight, Rebecca was drinking in the adjacent bar. When she passed him on her way to the Ladies, he envied her her glossy yellow parka, the supply of beer to which he had no access.

She returned from the toilet. She curled her lip. 'What does it feel like, being such a drongo?'

'I wish you'd change the record.'

'The arse is hanging out of your jeans.'

'Be cool,' said Ash, 'and shout us a jug.'

'Your skinny white arse is on display, Ashcan.'

She was gone for less than a minute. When she returned, she was holding a full glass. '"For what we are about to receive, make us truly thankful."' Standing on tiptoe, she emptied the contents of the glass all over his head.

He wore the fizzing, icy stream of ale. 'Thanks very much. What's your next trick?'

They found a taxi at the rank in Bond Street. There were golden saxophones in Shand Miller's window. Ash was conscious too of Rebecca's bag, its variously coloured scraps of suede. And when they got to Brooklyn and her flat, he saw that her bedspread was made out of scores of Peggy squares. Pinks and blacks predominated. Among the things she owned were a wee tin of Tiger Balm, a flash Bernina sewing machine and *The Third Eye* by Lobsang Rampa.

Her lashes printed shadows on her cheeks, tiny lilac forks. Yes, the tines of her lashes pierced you, hooking you securely. And oh how very major seemed her lavish nudity! 'Have you had many chicks, Ashley?'

'Never one as pretty as you.'

'I want your baby-seed. Squirt me full of baby-seed, sweetheart.'

Later she would claim that he'd given her her first proper climax. And that was how they first got together, in the days before young Ash began to drink in earnest.

60

Burning

'You haven't finished your soda pop,' says Ernest.

Scott glances out at the airfield. A silver airplane is waiting. Rain billows in across the tarmac, a huge fund of wetness falling from a great height.

Ernest frowns. 'This picture you're working on. What's it about?'

'It's a boxing picture for John Garfield.'

Ernest smiles. 'What do *you* know about boxing?'

'Not much. But I sat in a projection room and watched all the boxing pictures ever made.'

'All the boxing pictures ever made?'

'There's been a few. We're encouraged to *borrow* certain elements.'

'You don't say.'

'There are sources and we use 'em. I suppose it's like the Elizabethan theatre. Think of the London theatre of Shakespeare's day.'

'Drunkenness and plagiarism rife?'

Miss Craig returns from the buffet. Her nurse's uniform is largely hidden by her coat. Scott takes her hand, rubbing it as if to warm it up. 'Bid farewell,' he says, 'to Mister Hemingway.'

'It's been a pleasure,' says Ernest.

Scott dons his hat. A press photographer with a Speed-Graphic captures the moment, *pop*. 'Any message for your public, Mister Fitzgerald?'

In brown fedora and coat of beaver cloth, the scribe looks like a thinnish rodent begging. 'Miami's a swell town. I hope I'm able to drop by again.'

The props of the DC-3 are spinning, grinding the rain to a slipstream of mist. Fitzgerald and his nurse board the aircraft. 'You're acting kind of fishy,' says Miss Craig.

'The inside of a plane is very like a church.'

'I'll bet that damned beard slipped you a bottle.'

'I can almost see portholes of stained glass, little vases like stoups.'

The DC-3 takes off. The bottle of bourbon emerges from the coat. He's quiet at first, but soon a leaden malice clouds his eye. The difficulty is, it's nearly time to give him his injection. 'You've been so *good* of late,' the nurse ventures.

'Pressures build. I'm having a little slip.'

'Put that hooch away and try to get some sleep.'

'You won't want to give me my jab?'

'It's all right to skip it if you're resting.'

Anything to avoid a fuss. But the lightning and turbulence begin. She *knew* it would come to this. She watches him swig at his juice, the cunning Mister F, his eye gone as queer as an oyster. 'You're a good kid,' he says.

'Thank you.'

'You may be as glamorous as hell, but you're more than just another pretty face.'

'You sure are a charmer.'

'Why, certain women you meet, they're like a record with a blank on one side.'

'Really?'

The porthole is black—and then the incandescence of sheet lightning.

'I'm like a broken phonograph,' says Scott. 'From time to time I leak a scratchy tune.'

'Keep drinking and it's death. Death or insanity.'

'Before that comes a little mild success, a little mild failure. In Hollywood you get to see what *real* success buys you.'

The turbulence worsens. Scott struggles to get up, stands at last in the aisle with his bottle in his fist. 'I'd like a word with the pilot,' he tells the stewardess.

'The captain's got enough on his plate right now.'

'Sit down before you fall down,' says the nurse.

Scott changes colour now, a newt turning albino. The blood drains from his head—in an instant, utterly. 'Indulge me, honey. I want to see the cockpit.'

The plane bucks. Then plunges. Scott Fitzgerald comes a mighty cropper. The women pick him up, restore him to his seat. 'Don't chide me, please, Miss Craig.'

'I won't if you'll behave.'

'I once had capital. I once knew a great many stories, but I've told them all and now *I'm just like you.*'

'Don't kid yourself, buster.'

Scott leans back in his seat and closes his eyes. His girlish lip is moist, a violet Cupid's bow. It's rumoured that his wife's a troubled woman, passing her days in a leafy asylum. When God's lightning flares, it's almost like a

mad face at the porthole. The nurse thinks she can smell
something burning, fancies a lethal fire is somewhere being
kindled.

Liberty

Commander Byrd had just flown over the South Pole. The Graf Zeppelin was crossing the Atlantic regularly. As to Wall Street, well . . .

Paco's chief concern was to keep his grey suit pressed. He stood in the kitchen sans his jacket, waiting for the iron to get nice and hot. 'Steam from an iron. Who would have thought it?'

Rudolph was tuning his guitar. 'This impresses you?'

'This goes very deep,' the Spaniard told the busker. 'In all of Andalusia is nothing like this hissing appliance.'

A further cascade of junk mail hit the floor in the hall. Rudolph returned to the kitchen with his arms full of sticky-leaved brochures, mentholated chewing gum, sachets of hair conditioner. 'Of shit like this, embarrassing surfeit. While guys queue for soup and sleep in cardboard boxes!'

The Spaniard had begun to ply the iron. 'The lily have sleeves in which she hide her young.'

'What's *that* supposed to mean?''

But Paco had said what Paco had said. And the moon he saw that night on his way to work was a horse's skull chalkily drawn. It made him want to cram his mouth with chilled pebbles. For love of a Russian busker with blond hairs on his legs, I have abandoned much. But for the love of the blond hairs on the legs, I might have become a signwriter. A virtuoso of the brush. In the great tradition (no?) of Velázquez and Goya.

At Brooklyn Wesleyan, his first job was to trolley a stiff to the morgue. (Going in *there* earned you a few extra cents.) By the time he got back to Emergency, things were hotting up. Here you had it all, from burns and broken bones to strokes and heart attacks. Childbirth and dementia. Dog bites and the punctures made by human teeth. The bullet wounds came in two calibres: .38 and .45.

Clauson wore pink scrubs. Clauson did Demerol and clocked off on the dot. For the duration of his shift, however, Clauson worked with skill and compassion. 'Stand by to get ready, Paco. Some guy's on the loose in a McDonald's.'

'A disgruntled former employee?'

'They took back his dinky *tie* maybe.'

2 a.m. Into the gloomy bay downstairs, green-and-white ambulances began to roll. Such was the number of casualties, triage was attempted right there in the basement. Paco saw an injured cop from Alcohol, Tobacco and Firearms, a settler with an arrow through his sleeve, a brown charioteer all galled and spurned, his body a single messy wound. And Clauson was like: 'Can we make it snappy with that fucking plasma?'

The one just getting in and the other going out, Paco and Rudolph met at breakfast. Rudolph was wearing a skimpy towel bathrobe. How numerous and golden were the hairs on his legs! The shy Spaniard hoped to cop himself a feel, but the Russian seemed intent on continence.

Over bagels and coffee, they watched the television. Venting a blizzard of fluttering debris, a rocket climbed a tower. 'I'm expecting a call from Hollywood,' said Rudolph.

'From Hollywood. Of course.'

'You have some sort of problem with that?'

'Not me.'

'Disney are making the next James Bond. They dig the theme I wrote, they'll fly me to their Burbank studios.'

'Maybe they *like* your demo tape, maybe. But in Hollywood is avarice and cunning. Sipping at their green cigarettes, the mild demons gloat.'

'What's eating you, my sorrowful Paquito?'

'My heart trembles like the injured sea horse. America boasts docks and avenues and skyscrapers. America shows to the world nickel and tin foil, jazz and cocktails, but America is poor. New York is Senegal with machines. At bottom is only so much slime and wire. I make no allusion for the moment to those sinister boroughs in which living poets are jinxed by Chinamen and caterpillars.'

'You long for Asquerosa? Romilla?'

'Verily.'

On his way to work that night (snow had begun to totter down), Paco bought a copy of the *Saturday Evening Post.* Was Norman Rockwell greater than Velázquez? I've fallen for Mr Rockwell's pictures. Perhaps if I enrol again in classes . . .

To the hospital there came civilians deafened by bombs.

Innocents afflicted by necrotising fasciitis. Citizens fleeing lambent piles of waste and fizzing pools of chemicals. An astronaut checked in who confessed to having a small plastic Superman lodged in his rectum. 'Merry Christmas, Paco,' said Clauson.

'And to you the same, I'm sure.'

'Coming to the staff bash?'

'I'm holding this carotid closed at present.'

'New Year's Eve it is. There'll be lakes of ethanol. Stick with me and I'll get you hanged, kiddo.'

Not till 3 a.m. did Paco get a break. He drank a Coca-Cola and gazed out of a second-storey window. The slow snow of Brooklyn was puffed against hoardings, wafted through fake Gothic arches. Out there somewhere was Rudolph, busking for dimes even at this hour, waiting for Disney to ring him on his yellow Motorola. How glittery and blond the hairs on his legs, alas. And oh how Paco's heart pulsed like some transparent marine creature, some frilly, floaty thing made of jelly.

Running the Cutter

The house buckles and shrinks. No landlord ever visits.

Clint rises early. Using the mauve he found under the sink, he paints a bit more of the kitchen. Runs out of paint and goes out the back. Dabbles about at the tap in the yard, rinsing the brush and washing his hands.

He leaves the brush to soak in the ice-cream container. Makes a mug of coffee and takes it through to the bedroom. 'I'm off out, Kylie.'

She's feeding the baby. It's a funny little baby with tiny fingernails.

'We need more nappies, yes?'

'You'll notice I've left the Zip. The Zip and the doors I'll do a different colour.'

'Whatever,' says Kylie.

It's a humid sort of morning, brightly overcast. He never tucks his shirt in, not Clint. In baggy pants with pockets on the thighs, he's off to town and the house of Father Ambrose.

A fence of grey timber. Cabbage whites and monarchs duck and dive. And here's the spot where the other kid was murdered, stomped because he had the purple hair and the green fingernails.

The presbytery is full of Russian seamen. They sniff the sweet air of the harbour and jump ship. One inhabits a cupboard under the stairs. 'Help yourself to porridge,' says Father Ambrose.

'Where will your ministry take you today, Father?'

The good priest is Greek Orthodox. He was once an electrician from Petone. 'I have to take Yuri to the dentist. Also, there are voles in my beard. And I say unto you, Clinton—Would that these sad facts were otherwise.'

'Alvays the sod focts,' says Vlad, rolling the kid a cigarette.

Clint would like a job as an extra in a film. *Quiet on the set. That's lovely, Keanu. Cut* and *Check the gate* and *Print it, Melanie*.

Tim does the dishes at Fidel's. Aaron washes cop cars in the basement at Central. In a room at the back of a house on Walnut Street, Ho is building himself a time machine.

There's a rubble of electronic junk. From braided wires to pulse modulators, klystrons to cathode-ray oscilloscopes. Nothing is housed, you understand. And Ho's use of duct tape is famously promiscuous.

'How's it hangin, Ho?'

'I'm reconfiguring the joystick.'

'Trust me to barge right in.'

'I've begun to get a little sympathetic resonance. A wee touch of shiver in that second hemisphere.'

'Sounds gross.'

'Mine's black with two sugars. You'll see some Mallowpuffs.'

Clint fills the jug and switches it on. Changes the water

in the rat's cage. Humphrey seems well enough, but the room is lethal to flies. Flies venturing in from the garden and getting between the poles of Ho's array . . . They pop like pods, the fuckers.

It's proving to be a satisfactory outing. Returning to the streets, Clint checks his mental shopping list. Yes, the business of the day is now at hand—and for that you need a certain cool, a certain quiet flair. You have to believe in your own legitimacy, your own shining probity and worth. So it's straight up the aisle at Benchmark, willing yourself to feel a serene competence.

He scores a pail of high-gloss acrylic in Harem Tangerine. The superette will be more difficult. Grabbing up the Huggies will not be such a breeze.

He passes the spot where the other kid was topped, slippered till he bled from every orifice. He passes the brick shithouse, the magpies on the lawn of the war memorial—and knows he's on the home straight at last.

Kylie's up and about. She takes the Huggies from him silently. Then, 'Harem Tangerine? What sort of colour's that for a baby's digestion?'

'Ho's got buzzing in his hemispheres.'

'A nice beige would have done. A cinnamon or mushroom.'

'I'll pop out this arvo. I'll get us a food parcel from the Mission.'

Kylie changes the baby on the kitchen table. The female infant likes the look of Clint, scritching at his face with her teeny weeny nails. He presses his mouth to her tummy, blowing a series of flubby raspberries.

Nell Delaney

The city was an art-deco jewel. There were palms and cabbage trees, their shadows big black asterisks at noon. It seemed that at the end of every street were the esplanade and the sea. The blue ocean sparkled, an outrageous new brand of soft drink.

Nell was boarding with a Mrs Blades. Though her Holland blinds were fading, losing their stiffness to the glare without, the landlady kept a nice front room. A tall wireless hogged the floral carpet; Nell thought of it as looking pompous. Mrs Blades enjoyed the music of Eric Coates, the BBC's *Bandwagon*. 'Come and have a listen, dear,' she'd say—and sometimes Nell would join her for an hour.

It was only a five-minute walk to the Neptune. Nell liked the theatre's artsy chic, its rounded edges and low ceilings. And where but in an auditorium, the light from the screen a succession of lurid hues, could a girl feel so close to romance, so safely remote from it?

It was early in January. *Jesse James* would screen at eleven (it featured Henry Fonda and Tyrone Power). A canister of film under his arm, Sid the projectionist came through the foyer. 'The latest newsreel. Straight off the train.'

'You'd better get a move on,' said Nell.

'Did you hear him on the radio last night?'

'All in a lather again, I expect.'

'The German people labour under intolerable burdens. And Britain just keeps adding to them, according to Adolf.'

It was hard to know what to think. Mrs Blades doubted there'd be another war. Nell stuck to her torch and saved her shillings. Quite why she needed to save she couldn't have said, for she revelled in her work at the Neptune (in the ladies' musky scents, the men's cigarette smoke in buoyant layers) and felt she had a home with Mrs Blades. A wider view took in aquarium and skating rink, fronded avenue and balmy esplanade—and these things remained her very own discoveries, delights to which she lay a jealous claim.

On a Monday, Nell's day off, she liked to have her tea at the Waldorf Grill, then walk to the gardens and watch the sun go down. And when it got dark in the gardens, the lights came on. It was as if the theatrical lamps hidden in the shrubbery took over from nature, prolonging the slow pyrotechnics of the setting sun. She'd sit on a bench and light a cigarette, content to feel content.

'It's as warm as toast tonight, don't you think?'

She looked at the man with small interest. 'I can't think *what* it's as warm as. We could do with a breath of wind, I suppose.'

'Exactly,' said the man. 'A zephyr's what we need.'

The red boles and the purple. And where a hidden lamp was green, the leaves it lit took on a semblance of wetness, an extra and artificial greenness. Not really wanting to make conversation, Nell voiced a few inconsequential thoughts, talking of summer showers and steaming pavements.

The man continued to stand. 'I like to see a woman holding a cigarette. You're an usherette at the Neptune, aren't you? A bit of a waste, if you don't mind my saying. The fact of the matter is, you've a lovely speaking voice. Have you ever thought about going in for dramatics?'

His name was Cyril Cole. If he favoured cravats and cricketer's trousers, he wasn't as pretty as other sissies she'd known. His features were smooth and brown and slant—like those of a Mongol herdsman. Nell came to think of him as having been marred in the womb. He'd been tanned by a force beamed through his mother's waters. Tinkered with and queered by polarising rays.

They met for lunch the following Monday. The Carlton's dining room was a place of many mirrors. 'When you've finished your ice cream, I'd like to show you my studio,' he said.

'Let me guess. You photograph babies?'

'I work in radio. I'm the man behind the serial *Hal Burke, Detective.*'

Flat-roofed and coral pink, a building near the beach. The studio itself was lined with cork tiles. Nell looked at all the kindergarten gadgets for making sound effects. She felt affronted by the free-standing door—a door to nothing, a door leading nowhere. 'Heavens,' she said, dismayed.

Cyril was holding a pistol. 'This is where it all happens. I've brought you to the heart of the enterprise. Hal Burke stands right here at the key mike.'

'"Grab your hat, Troy."'

'I'm what they call a producer. I sit in that booth over

there. I twiddle knobs and cue the various effects—the sound of a motor boat or soda siphon.'

'The crack of a gun going off?'

'Whatever the script calls for.'

Nothing stirred in her. Nor had she seen the last of him: he turned up at Mrs Blades' that evening. The landlady had gone upstairs; the 'Knightsbridge March' was spilling from the pompous wireless. 'Please forgive the lateness of the hour, but I had to see you again.'

'Whatever for, Mister Cole?'

'The writers feel that Hal needs a fiancée. I'm hoping to persuade you to audition for the part.'

Nell had a weakness for motorcars. Cyril's stood at the kerb, as shiny and black as pooled ink, its spare wheel seated in a slot in the running-board. He drove with a maidenly primness—out of town and along the coast to a spot above the sea. Nell remembered the door in the studio, the door that led nowhere. 'I hadn't thought you'd stop. Was stopping such a great idea?' she asked.

'It's a good place for seeing shooting stars.'

'Oh.'

He turned in his seat and touched her fichu. 'Forgive me. I seem to be forgetting myself. It's just that my heart is full of the most tremendous regard for you.'

She knew a cliché when she heard one. 'Eyes forward, Cole.'

'I'm in a state of awe. You've rocked me well and truly. I'm feeling as I've never felt before, for anyone.'

His tanned face looked glossy and taut, as if made of plastic. Nell removed his hand from her knee. 'Do *you* think Chamberlain's kidding himself?'

'I can't wear khaki, I know that much.'

'The air force might be more your cup of tea. You could grow a nice moustache.'

'"So young and so untender?" Your prattle's killing me.'

She didn't pity him. She *couldn't* pity him. On still nights like this, the Nazis rallied at Nuremberg. She supposed the dewy grass wet Hitler's boots. 'Are you going to drive me home, or shall I get out and walk?'

Red Shifts

1

Fluorescent mice have colonised the sewers. As robots tend their spectral dynamos, rain streams from the beaks of gryphons. A senior citizen walks in off the street and asks to see a detective. Dimple-chinned Brett Chandler conducts the whiffy gent to an office on Level 30. 'What's eating you, grandad?'

'It was many years ago.'

'You donned a Groucho mask and snatched a purse?'

'I murdered an attractive meter maid.'

'So take your time,' says Brett, 'and run it by me slowly.'

Further assertions are made, tested guilefully, advanced afresh. It's not long before the air is blue with cigarette smoke. 'Any chance of a brew? I'm getting as parched as a mummy's twat, sat here.'

'A mummy's twat, Tommy? Was there any call to sully the ambience?'

'You've swished my lighter, Brett. That's my BiC you've got, I think you'll find.'

'I *do* beg your pardon. I end up with pockets full of crap.'

'It's easily done. My *word* yes.'

'I'm like an Electrolux. There's not a Biro safe.'

'We'll say no more about it. It's just that the green ones are hard to come by.'

2

Brett rents a room in a quiet rooming-house. Lives on instant noodles and bananas. Stirs slices of banana into his curried glop. Immerses himself in the fiddly task of building a Halifax bomber. (You need a *range* of paints is what you need. The tiny cans are floral in their variety.)

Brett is sometimes visited by Claude. Claude works for Pacific Dent Service. The two men get drunk on tequila, cheat one another at cards, swap wrist-watches.

Claude visits once too often. Surfacing the following morning, Brett is bent and mystified and craves demulcent fluids. Alone and of his own initiative, he drinks a little beer and smokes a little toot. Yes, he gets a little fucked and descends to a crypt beneath a dental clinic. The Twelve Steps scroll is central; glossy posters depict molars wearing pants, glasses of milk with eyelashes.

'My name is Brett and I hate these meetings and all who sail in them.'

On top of all of which, the job and its demands. Blue-eyed Brett Chandler and his partner, Stahr, raid a gallery down by the marina. The paintings feature pyramids, flying saucers and tumescent pricks. 'The mayor wants you closed,' Brett tells the curator. 'Anything to offer by way of mitigation, Mister . . . ?'

'Gysin. Brion Gysin.'

'Are you by any chance the reclusive author of *The Last Museum*?'

'He is,' says Grace Jones, all clavicle and cleavage.

'Forth from its nest,' says Gysin, 'the evening staggers. It seems we're busted good, though our vices be imperfect.'

Stahr is chewing gum. 'What's it *like* to be a genius?'

3

The nights continue wet. Downpipes rupture and awnings collapse.

Out at Bamboo Airport, big silver pods atomise the rain. As our weary hero is grinding a perp's face into the tarmac, the sucker's ray gun discharges.

The following Sunday, Brett gets a little fucked and goes to a meeting at Trades Hall. 'He caught me in the foot. He made of my shoe a tattered, smoking thing.'

'It's simple,' says the chairman. 'Just don't pick up a drink.'

'That rotten perp,' says one of the ladies present.

Her name is Leilani (does a sweeter one exist?) and the brown globe of her shoulder has a certain shine to it. She knows what it is to have a bandaged foot. She plucks a speck of lint from the sleeve of Brett's jacket; she walks him back to his rooming-house but two blocks distant.

He's obliged to her, is Brett. Would she like to see his flock of pretty warplanes?

She thinks not.

Could she go a banana milkshake?

Another time, perhaps. But she kisses him on the cheek, does Leilani, her lips as cool as a sable brush, and Brett forgets for a moment the ticking of life's meter, the pitiless drip drip drip of life's accreting judgements.

Brindle Embers

The halls of the palace were deserted. Father Lipatti sought an unmarked door next to that of Treasury. The office he entered was absurdly narrow. Its single tall window admitted a glacial light. The chocolate-coloured linoleum had everywhere been blackly cicatrised by smouldering cigarette butts.

To the side of the desk jammed in against the window sat Colonel Stok. His long leather coat buttoned at the throat, he pinged with his fingernail the pear-shaped bottle standing beside the lofty, ornate, chimerical typewriter. 'A drop of slivovitz, my dear Vasile?'

'Thank you,' said the priest. 'The streets are treacherous. There are slicks of black ice.'

'You need new boots,' said Stok, '—that much is obvious.'

'And my funk and malleability—are they apparent also?'

Before Stok could answer, the journalist whose office this was returned. Sepia-cheeked and wispy of moustache, this bibulous hack was known as the Tartar. 'So much for trying to coax some heat out of the boiler.'

'Please,' said the Colonel. 'No need to tell us where you've been. Being utterly corrupt, you're perfectly trustworthy. If you have that film to hand, I'll trouble you to pass it to Father Lipatti here.'

'If I must,' said the Tartar.

'But of course you must,' said Stok.

The Tartar opened the nethermost drawer in his desk and brought forth a small, zincy-looking canister. 'And much good may it do you,' he said, handing the tube to the priest.

'Father Lipatti dreams of an end to shortages. An end to dearth of bread and medicines and boots. Isn't that so, Vasile?' asked the Colonel.

'I do more than dream. And when I'm caught you'll throw me to the wolves.'

Stok's face remained unsmiling. As he filled three murky tumblers with plum brandy, his leather coat creaked like a pine tree, a burdened loft. 'It will never come to that. I hope and pray it will never come to that.'

The film secreted beneath his soutane, Father Lipatti walked toward the tram. This down-at-heel priest with his failed youth club, his sexual difficulties, his bag of cankered apples—was he being followed? Vasile thought not. In the weird gloom of four in the afternoon, the globes of the streetlamps seemed to house dim brindle embers. A not-unpleasant stink of burning tyres was added to the sugary miasma surrounding the boiled-sweet factory.

Iron wheels and iron bells. A brute, compacting cold. Alighting from the tram outside Our Lady of the Rosary, Father Lipatti passed the sacristy, the wooden campanile, the cabbage patch with grubby scraps of ice littering its furrows, and let himself into the presbytery through a back door. Here was the room, formerly a sort of conservatory, in which Vasile had attempted to meet and entertain the kids of the parish. To the wall not made of glass there still adhered posters concerning acne and smoking, alcohol and heroin, condoms and STDs. But the place had thrice been burgled, the electric heater stolen, seismic Martian tags jaggedly indited . . .

In the hall at the front of the house, he donned his overcoat. From the study he uplifted his Mass kit, a book-sized wallet. *Lead us not into temptation, but deliver us from evil.* The habit of prayer died hard, but was it merely habit?

With the kit in his coat pocket, he left the presbytery. A second tram conveyed him to an orphanage on the outskirts of the city. He hadn't left behind the bag of apples Stok had given him; when Zelea had looked at the brown and wormy fruit, the stunned director tried to rise to the occasion. 'Shall I take you to little Georges, Father?'

'I don't want to see him. I can't bear to see him.'

'He returns himself to a state of resignation—of blankness, if you will—and then his drunken aunt reappears, galvanising in the child memories that had almost been extinct.'

'Hard as it is to watch, it's not for you to prevent.'

The men were standing in the doctor's ill-equipped office. Where countless heads of greasy hair had brushed them, the walls bore a sort of high-water mark. 'Apples,' said the haggard Zelea. 'What am I to do with a few withered apples? At brave academies in better times, I was introduced to the words "kwashiorkor" and "marasmus".

They denote conditions sharing many features. They imply anaemia, diarrhoea, lethargy. They mean failure to grow and susceptibility to infection.'

Give us this day our daily bread. Morning and eve, the same feeble mantra.

'The orphanage is always in our prayers. In mine and those of my parishioners.'

Night had long since fallen. Projected by the office window, a strawy light made visible the cloister and courtyard without. A female attendant was sloshing the contents of a bucket down a drain. Her massive bust was shapeless; her huge hips appeared to give her pain. She was wearing a babushka and a great long soiled apron. Now crumpled, less than elfin, her cherry-red booties had once had pointed toes. She looked to the priest like some doomed, squamous, insect-eating beast; he imagined her to be inadequate, surlily wilful, far from entirely kind. As she lumbered back toward the main block, Father Lipatti pictured little Georges, his shaven head and tiny shoulders, his round eyes like those of a loris. And Vasile pictured too (could almost smell) the capacious freezer that was the dormitory, the cots with their bars of enamelled dowelling, the urine-soaked mattresses so hard to dry, the nappied and ill-clad children of both sexes, just as mute and watchful as their battered cohorts elsewhere.

Doctor Zelea spoke again. 'Shall I list the things we need? Apart from drugs? We need linen and soap and disinfectant. We need clean water. We need onions and barley and potatoes, to say nothing of salt and flour. Anything you can give us, we already need.'

But Father Lipatti was thinking of bears. Bears made

psychotic by tether and cage. The white ones prevented from roaming snow and ice.

Zelea sat down in his broken typist's chair. His desk was innocent of charts and prescription forms. 'I close my mind to the whole disgraceful mess. There were doctors in the SS, you know. Physicians who became mere instruments. And worse.'

Vasile roused himself. 'Rrok the market gardener is bringing cabbages. Beetroot too, if I'm not mistaken. Would you like to join me in prayer for just a minute?'

He drank a cup of coffee at the kiosk on the platform, then caught the train for K__. Young and slender-hipped, the guard stalked up the carriage like a circus performer on a tightrope, then punched the cleric's green-and-orange ticket without a word. How much like a child's anticipation of the plenteous novelties of Christmas were one's own sexual longings! *If a kingdom is divided against itself, that kingdom cannot stand.* But Father Lipatti mastered himself with an inner exertion as practised as harsh.

It had been snowing in K__. Outside the station, a cab was waiting with its headlights shining; the priest avoided it and set out for the village on foot. He hadn't gone far when the taxi caught up with him and slowed to a crawl. With an old grey Mercedes inching along beside him, Vasile decided to speak. 'I prefer to walk,' he called.

'Get in, Father.'

His blood an icy sludge, he craved sugar, fire, certainty. He was sick of responsibility, of having to be brave. He'd had it to the teeth with having to be principled, courageously alert while remaining unconvinced and tepid. In this bleak

Wonderland, conviction was stupid and bravery gutless. That zincy-looking canister of film riding in the pocket of his shirt was making a target of his heart. A gambler to whom it had all become too much, he did as he'd been told and got into the cab.

Vasile had never seen the driver before. 'Should I know you from somewhere?'

'The barber's disappeared. I'm to drive you to the lake.'

'Take me to the border. I'll make the run myself.'

'Is that what Colonel Stok would want?'

Rule One: Never deny merely knowing an agent. Rule Umpteenth: Silence is always an option.

'The lake is nice in summer,' said the driver. 'In winter by night is not so good maybe.'

They were met by a man equipped with an Astra machine-pistol. 'Get out of the car with your hands above your head, priest.'

A Wonderland indeed. The rusting tin signs and obsolete bowsers of an abandoned petrol station. To one side of the garage, a copse of birches the recent snow had prettified, black and white and tan in the lights of the Mercedes. Holding his Mass kit in his left hand, Father Lipatti emerged from the vehicle.

The man with the gun advanced. 'What's this you're showing me?'

'I wasn't meaning to draw attention to it.'

The officer in charge seemed simply to materialise. Looking every inch the secret policeman (an obdurate presence completing the ambush), he wore a leather overcoat like Stok's. 'Show us what you have in the wallet, padre.'

The gunman gave Vasile quite a shove. 'Do as the major says!'

This was how it began, then. In unpleasantness and pushing. 'An ordination present from my uncle. Tools of the trade, as it were. Just the few things needed if and when . . .'

The gunman brought his Astra down with force, knocking the wallet and its contents out of the priest's hands. Miniature cruets and plinthed crucifix, paten and chalice and stole—they spilled like so much loot across the snow. And Father Lipatti imagined himself kneeling, gathering the consecrated vessels to himself. In fact, lamentably, he moved not a muscle.

'Film,' said the major. 'I don't see any film.'

A coward's piquant shame. And yet one did one's best, even finding nerve enough to say, 'And what film might *that* be?'

The Boiler House

It's the Age of Aquarius. The longer your hair, the sexier. Sandals and flared jeans, that's me.

'Please Respect the Privacy of Patients.' I register the place in terms of roses and tennis courts, asphalt paths and beamed ceilings. From a window at the back of Rutherford, one can see a little mortuary.

'Do you dream about drinking?' Sir Charles Burns asked. I did and do and now there's something wrong with my heart. A drink would fix my heart; a drink is not exactly contraindicated.

I'm learning to polish floors with a machine. Tilting the handles gets you traction and momentum. Calm, surcease, belonging. The rocking swing and shush of the polisher. I'm nonetheless the thirstiest man in Australasia.

As my father and I approached Rutherford, a man came out to meet us. 'I'm the Ward Host.' He shook my father's hand. 'Welcome to Queen Mary, Mister Cochrane.'

'You've got the wrong bloke,' my father said.

A diffuse rain fell, wafting down like steam. On my first night in Hanmer, scents sulphurous and piney. From the tables in the hall came a clacking of balls. The light in the boiler house suggested a course of action: when my treatment was over, I'd get a job shovelling coal. Faulkner had had his post office, I'd have my boiler house.

Dr Maling is as leggy as a flamingo. 'Has it ever occurred to you that drinking is a sort of petulance?'

'?'

'A way of saying *I want it all*?'

It has and does but now there's something wrong with my heart. I put away my polisher and go to breakfast. Sunlight fills the dining room. The surly Belfast man offers to trim my hair. I follow him to his room and he seats me in a chair. Snips away for a while before announcing, 'I've given you a choice of styles, now tell me which you prefer.'

One side of my head retains its brown curls, the other has been almost completely denuded.

It's a glorious day in February. I feel big-eared and stark. Warmth and clarity, the odour of mown grass—and now I look like everyone else. I sport travesty: my shorn condition seems to represent compromise and moral slippage. A man in his sixties tells me, 'An ignorant sort of a prick, that Belfast sod.'

The lunch bell rings. One's place at table is dictated by a seating plan. A bag of toffees and a telegram have been left beside my knife. 'BEST WISHES ON YOUR TWENTY-FIRST LOVE MUM AND DAD.' The telegram read and internalised, there remains the mystery of the sweets, the provocation of the toffees.

Wonders

I once worked for an Indian fruiterer, washing carrots and parsnips in a concrete tub full of icy water. Those were the days of coal, gas, Yorkshire pudding, rosaries, saveloys, scapulae, buttery toast and Marmitey mushrooms.

The city boasted then a floral clock. Our mother cut up old sheets, hemming them on the Singer to make us handkerchieves. Every now and then, the piano sidled into the middle of the living room.

Times change, of course. Stukkas plunge, a mustang bolts. Hundreds of snakes with their mouths sewn shut are confiscated by officials. My Goldair heater begins to self-destruct, the filament combusting with a dazzling white light. My dropsheets resembling Jackson Pollocks, I do out Stella's flat in mint and aubergine. She lights a candle here, a cone of incense there. She drinks and drinks (Chianti) and gets incredibly pissed. She sticks her chin out like Gregory Peck and slugs me.

Whence comes the myth that the bully is a coward?

*

I retreat to my own crummy pad. When a bus stops outside, my few knives and forks shiver in their drawer. Sympathetic resonance. And I fall to thinking of all the lesser women, the ladies who never became a fixture, the chicks I bedded for a night or two in winter, when the world and I were young. There was Rosalind, for instance. To whom I tried to get married late one evening, whisking her up to the monastery in a cab. The hip Redemptorist we roused from his cell declined to officiate.

And then there was the redhead with the bulging eyes. Hyperthyroidism? Hypothyroidism? What was her name, for God's sake?

And what of Audrey?

And what of Isabel?

And what of the first photograph I ever took, with my uncle's Kodak, a box camera with a focal range of 3ft to infinity, of a bison, of a bison at the zoo, a single hapless bison?

Sprats rain down on the fishing port of Great Yarmouth. Air Rarotonga takes delivery of a Saab 340. My eye comes up nicely, adopting all the opalescent hues of a paua shell.

A night and a morning pass before Stella drops in. She's wearing her slinky leather strides. She flushes the toilet twice, noisily. She opens the fridge and glares at the bare shelves. 'They're not exactly groaning with provender, Smith.'

'It's just as well you've brought a little something.'

She drags from her Just Jute bag olives, salami and Gorgonzola. Also, a bottle of Chianti. 'Do you fancy anything?'

I tell her I'll have a cup of tea.

Stella *completely fills* the electric jug. 'Have you found that stencil you promised me?'

'The fleur-de-lis? I'll have to have a bit of a rummage.'

'And when are you coming back? To do the stencilling?'

'When I'm good and ready, girl.'

'Ah. So now the worm is on the other foot. I get it.'

'I wish you hadn't come here in those slinky leather pants.'

'Don't point that eye at me.'

'I'm totally drooling, woman. I'm utterly captive to your yummy liquorice legs.'

'Cool it, Smith,' says Stella.

My brother has me to dinner at the Duxton. Miles is a geologist. He's in town to deliver a paper on drilling protocols, rules of his own formulation. The quiet tie and plain white shirt belie his breadth of mind. The trim dark beard detracts not a whit from the warmth of his smile.

We dine on lamb cutlets and bread-and-butter pudding. Our repast concluded, Miles shows me his room. There's a fine view of the harbour below (intriguing lights slide across the black water) and a screen on which to watch the in-house porn. I'd be perfectly willing to live in this room for the rest of my life.

Though he fails to recall my snapshot of that single, hapless bison, Miles and I enjoy a convivial chat.

Taking stencil and gold paint, I return to Stella's pad. Frank Sinatra is singing, *When somebody loves you / It's no good unless he loves you / All the way.*

Stella has been reading *Growing Up in New Guinea.* 'We're

strangers to ourselves, you and I.'

'I never doubted it.'

Stella has been visiting a medium in Doctors Common. For twenty lousy bucks, she gets to converse with an ancient Persian magus. 'He says he can sense that I'm understimulated.'

'It sounds as if he knows his onions, then.'

Have I mentioned the fact that spring is upon us? For she of the leather trousers and skirts, I run little errands in the bright forenoons. Putting stencilling behind me, I replace all the washers in her taps. Refreshed and empowered by a course of aromatherapy, Stella is now partaking of nothing stronger than seltzer and hock.

Sparrows scuffle on the roof of her sunporch. She gives me instruction in how to caress her, how to stroke her vulva in such a way as to ready her for sexual intercourse.

She says, 'I hope one day to teach at an ivy-clad college.'

'You'll make a fine teacher.'

'I somehow *know* I shall.'

'You guide *my* hand in all I do.'

'Quite so, you rigid hunk.'

The cherry trees are putting forth crinkly pink blossoms. A letter written by Jesus turns up in a motel room in Boise, Idaho. And Stella no longer addresses me as 'Smith'.

Blue Lady

One day in July, stepping off the bus at Courtenay Place, his legs almost buckled under him. He was weak-kneed and shaky, his insides felt all dithery and flummoxed, but he drew the line at sitting down on the pavement. Rigidly determined to buy his grog and return to his flat, he moved forward unsteadily. The gloomy bottlestore had mock-Spanish arches; he filled his flagon from a 'barrel' of sweet sherry. His starveling's metabolism could only deal with the sweet stuff. He needed the food of sugar, sugar in frequent liquid doses.

1989, the weather vile. His flat faced Wakefield Park, affording him a view of pines, drainage ditches, rugby posts like gallows. On the boggy, puddled fields, throngs of gulls huddled like routed troops; perhaps they mirrored his own inconsequential defeat. His probation officer had found him the flat, extracted him from the rooming-house in which he'd lived for the past crepuscular decade. 'A fresh start,' the officer had said, '—but now we've got to work on drying you out, Ashley.'

He hadn't seen the busy probie since. Rain came off the

strait in icy, parcelled whumps. At his window above the park, Ashley sometimes heard the voices of groundsmen and golfers, the tramp of sprigged shoes on the gravel below. Beyond the line of pines at the western edge of the park, bits of the Home of Compassion were visible. And Ashley himself had once been put in there—for yet another detox, of course. He remembered the pretty nun in charge of his Hemineurin and generous with it. He remembered the whiteness, the clean sheets, the plaster saints on pedestals, the numinous and healing atmosphere. There'd been no one else in his quiet little ward, and he'd felt like a character in one of Hemingway's stories.

Could he do it all again, for the umpteenth time? He doubted it and dreaded having to try. He was too far gone to find the nerve to quit, too sick to marshal the necessary forces. And yet he could conceive of being sober, project his thoughts toward an idyll of sobriety, however remote and unlikely.

The flat remained shadowy and bare, furnished with only a pot, a chair, a bed. His portable typewriter stayed in its zippered grey cover. Nor did Ashley want the clutter of superfluous objects, the burden of ownership. He was in his fortieth year; if this new pad of his meant quiet and privacy at last, it had come too late, too late. In his booze-softened bones, he knew that he knew it: he wouldn't be staying long.

It was as if a sort of countdown had begun. In some elusive sense, these were the last days. Yes, this was the beginning of the end; there was something apocalyptic in the light; the dull, dirty sky looked moronic. In spite of all of which, Ashley must endure. Every afternoon, he took the bus as far as Courtenay Place in order to fill a bottle or a flagon. Returning to the flat one particular afternoon, he saw that his typewriter had been set up on the kitchen bench. Typed on a page torn from an exercise book, a note had been left in the machine. 'Dear Ash, I let in some blokes with some furniture for you. Regards, Fred.'

Fred was the block's 'custodian', a glorified caretaker with keys to every padlock and door. But just who'd sent this load of ugly junk (a couple of fat armchairs, a hulking great wardrobe and a daintily useless escritoire) remained a mystery until that evening, when Fred dropped by. Young and lean and brown, the caretaker was wearing a tool belt and holding a can of beer. 'The guy who drove the truck said his name was Garth. Told me you'd be grateful for a chair or two.'

'I wish you'd kept him out.'

'I thought he was a mate of yours.'

'He is.'

'But you'd sooner do without this crap he's dragged up here?'

'How am I supposed to get rid of it?'

Fred hadn't shaved in a while. 'This place smells like a dental clinic.'

'That'll be the methylated spirits. I've been doing some cleaning.'

Dense with pliers and screwdrivers, Fred's tool belt sagged like some overelaborate codpiece. 'Cool. No worries. I stick to the ale myself.'

The following morning, Ashley woke to find that he'd drunk all the sherry in the place. He'd long been adept at getting and staying drunk. Where drinking was concerned, there was no room for sloppiness or error, for less than scrupulous practice; now, his failure to anticipate his own egregious needs was forcing him to breakfast on meths and tap water. He couldn't drink water at the best of times, but the taste of meths unlaced by sherry or soft drink . . . was nothing short of emetic. He sat on his straight-backed chair and sweated and retched. He sat with his only pot between his knees . . . and spewed into the pot. *This is nowhere*, he thought, *this is the fucking pits.*

His nose ran. His eyes streamed. At about ten that morning, someone knocked gently at his door. How dire a sound those polite knuckles made! Ashley didn't want a further dose of Fred; he didn't *want* more jumbo furniture. And sat tight until the knocker went away.

The pub on The Parade would soon be opening. It beckoned like a hospital. But Ashley hadn't been in Island Bay since leaving it for good some twenty years ago. He'd return as a fit and moneyed adult, a chap wafted in off an oilrig. No. In a soft ancient parka smelling like tar, he'd return as the insect he was—a mutilate and twitching stick insect.

He wiped his eyes and tidied himself. He pocketed what remained of his cash. As he climbed the scabby drive to the road, his legs felt rickety and unsafe. Walking down the long hill toward Antarctica, he could think of nothing but alcohol's beneficence, its horrible absence from his system. With the firemen's training school in sight, however, he passed a spot reminding him of something: the tram crash in which he'd been slightly injured as a boy. His cocky penchant for riding on trams had been smashed out of him. *Thirty years later, I live on cigarettes and fusel oil; I dream of cafeteria meals of sausages and mashed potatoes and gravy; the ghost of an old neuropathy buzzes in my calves.*

By the time he reached the tavern, Ashley was cold and wet. He felt like an ill-rehearsed actor. He'd comb his sopping hair and make his entrance—but would he be served? Tremulous and pale and stupefied by need, he was scared of bumping into anyone he knew—some cobber of his dad's from way back when, for instance.

Tiffany lamps. A carpet of purple and gold. This was a lounge on a 'neighbourhood' scale, its patrons numbering fewer than a dozen. Repairing to the men's, Ashley dried his face on the roller towel, tried to warm his hands under the blower. He'd emerged from the toilet and was making his way to the bar when someone addressed him. 'I'd know you anywhere, Venus.'

Seated at a table with a pint in front of him, Toby McRae was dressed in civvies. Perhaps the fish-eye lens of Ashley's vision magnified the breadth of the policeman's knees. 'Just my luck,' said Ashley, 'I *crawl* in here for a quiet bloody gin . . .'

'Relax. It's good to see you.'

'You're putting on the beef, McRae. Still playing footy?'

'Packed *that* in years ago.'

'I guess you did. We're not getting any younger. It's just that I remember you at college, thumping your chest and breaking pates.'

'Only on the paddock.'

'Only on the paddock. I never dreamed you'd become a cop. There wasn't enough of the bully in you.'

McRae smiled a bleak, defensive smile. He was probably unused to indulging civilians. 'Nice of you to say so. What are you up to these days?'

The question was brutally well meant. Policemen and priests: they never seemed quite 'of the world' to Ashley. 'What am I up to? I'm drinking myself to death is what I'm up to.'

'A slow process?'

'A *very* slow process.'

'Tried AA?'

'I've tried everything.'

'And you know about the warrant?'

'What warrant's that?'

'There's a warrant out for your arrest.'

'But I'm on probation. My probie's meant to *orch*estrate these things.'

'Surrender yourself. Get yourself police bail. An hour in the cells, tops.'

Pinch me here and now. Make a couple of phone calls and have me driven to a place of white walls and clean sheets and plaster saints on pedestals. And the right medication, of course: fat yellow caps of Hemineurin, the queen of sedatives. 'Nice to catch up, Toby. Maybe I'll do as you suggest. Just at the moment though, that bar's looking pretty damned attractive.'

'Enough said, Ashley.'

To one side of the servery stood a young man in jeans, a builder's tape-measure clipped to his belt. A regular, obviously. The coast being clear, Ashley fronted the barmaid. 'A double gin with just a squirt of tonic. But no ice. Please.'

The girl busied herself. With two or three doubles inside him, Ashley could begin to function. But as he waited for his life-saving drink, he felt bilious, faint, disorientated; his anxiety threatened to throw him to the floor in an epileptic fit, stop his heart and close him down for keeps.

The barmaid slid a glass in his direction. 'Cheers.'

Ashley paid the cynical sum demanded. It was only when he'd picked up the glass that he saw the gelid rubble it contained. 'You've put ice in this. I particularly asked you not to put ice in my drink.'

'Oops. I'll try and remember next time.'

'Are you simply incapable of simply . . . ?'

'I've *said* I'm sorry.'

'Listen, you cloth-eared bint. Not everybody likes . . . *gar*lic on their steak. Not everybody wants . . . *lumps* in their medicine.'

'You've made your point,' said the regular, the guy with the tape measure clipped to his belt.

'But have I?'

'Get over it. Grow up. You're behaving like a big girl's blouse.'

100

Programmed Maintenance

Angela gives blood, has her teeth cleaned by a dentist on The Terrace, likes to visit the High Court during dodgy murder trials. Every now and then, she travels to Kaikoura to watch the whales. (Those whales are something else: by means of ESP, they're able to swap 3D images.)

She's tired of being mauled and prodded. She's sick of being put to the pork sword. For the next little while, she'll deny herself the privilege of being ejaculated into. (You guessed it: her last affair ended badly, in mutual contempt.)

Her body remains trim and firm, touch wood. She's always been proud of her breasts. Nor is she ashamed of her artistic bent. As a self-employed window-dresser, she services pharmacies on a programmed-maintenance basis. She always gives a window fizz and flavour, visiting upon it a Christmassy renaissance of tinsel and glitter and styrofoam pebbles, whatever the season. Working in stockinged feet, she revels in the scents of Coppertone and Ponds, Canoe and Imperial Leather.

*

She owns a smallish house in Newtown. Relaxing after work, she'll smoke a third of a number, sip at a bourbon and Coke with plenty of ice in it. She'll put on *West Side Story* (the soundtrack of the film) and listen to Marni Nixon singing *When love comes/ So strong/ There is no right or wrong/ Not a* think *I can do . . .*

Her mornings are subdued, even sorrowful. From the window of her front room, she can look across the road to a kiddies' playground. Behind the still swings is a hill dense with trees and shrubs. Can it be a tui that Angela hears chiming? Her Pentax binoculars have a powdery, matt-grey finish. She focuses on the kowhai; a trio of wax-eyes is brought before her by the stealthy magnetism of strong lenses.

One of her neighbours is a scruff. A long-toed, gingery scruff. She catches him eating fish and chips on the steps between their houses. (These lichened, pitted steps have a dated grandeur. Though entirely hers by rights, all the students use them.) 'Hi,' she says, 'my name is Angela.'

'I'm Totally Slutted,' she hears him reply.

In the days that follow, she learns this much: his friends call him Tom. He works on his Cortina in bare feet. The vehicle is painted black and white in shabby imitation of an American police car (there's even a bogus shield on the driver's door). When Angela next thinks about 'doing it', she seems to be seeing ginger dreadlocks, legs lean and pale, denim shorts with ragged, wispy hems.

The first week of December brings a warm and rainy night. Angela has put her rubbish out. Descending to the road, she rids herself of yet another bag of soup cans and eggshells and crushed milk cartons. The birds on the hill are silent. The lukewarm rain pelts down, as silvery as that in an old British film. And Angela pauses, glad of her umbrella, and sees what she has always been going to see.

Like the ghost of some brave Spitfire pilot, Tom is standing a pace or two away. 'I was going to doss in the car again tonight.'

'*Were* you?'

His face is very wet. 'They've edged me out of the pad. I haven't been paying my whack.'

'You look like a drowned rat.'

He explains that the Cortina doesn't go, is likely to remain forever stationary. 'I walk about till late. I'm just getting *in*, so to speak.'

And so it comes about that Tom is brought inside, lies in a volume of hot green water, wraps himself in Angela's bathrobe.

He stands in her front room in a robe too short for him. She drapes his wet things across a clothes horse. The sodden jeans give off a sweetish, penile odour. 'You should have washed your hair.'

'Maybe,' says Tom.

'All those kinky braids. You'd have to unwind them, I expect.'

'It's a whole huge performance.'

'Never mind. So what are you studying at polytech?'

'Information technology.'

'I've no idea what *that's* all about.'

'Me neither.'

He sits on Angela's sofa and eats morosely a cheese-and-chutney sandwich. He's a no-hoper, clearly—but with long, sexy toes by Michelangelo. His knees of mauve and white look delicate, equine. A knee has two components, like an 8 or an egg-timer.

Angela stands before him feeling all hot and bothered. 'I don't go in for kids half my age, and I certainly don't go in for skinny redheads.'

'Of course not,' says Tom.

'I haven't been treated well by men. *I haven't been treated well!*—incredibly.'

Tom puts his plate aside. Rises from the sofa. Lets the bathrobe fall.

His chest is wide and flat, as if drawn by Jean Cocteau. On the undersides of his forearms, the big veins are forked like bolts of lightning.

Thinks Angela: What is a man's body, if not a visual feast? Thinks Angela: His navel seems to dribble pubic hair, a trickle of wee Xs. Can this be the guy I'll never forget and measure all others against?

The Tenant

I died in 1986 at the age of thirty-five. The clinical notes mention respiratory arrest, *grand-mal* convulsion, cardiac arrest. The clinical notes mention intravenous steroids, Aminophylline, nebulised Salbutamol, Augmentin. 'The patient was deeply cyanosed and required intubation and paralysis.' 'His sputum grew haemophilus influenzae.'

Cyanosed.

The woman in the next flat along is an ideal neighbour. No music, no parties, no men. I never hear a peep, except when she's using her spin-drier. She's off to work at eight every morning, having slept the sleep of the just—the perfumed, pinkish sleep of the asexual. Nor is she unattractive.

Charlie. If things were otherwise, I might take an interest myself. If things were otherwise, there's *much* I might take an interest in. I'd like to learn to weld or drive a fire engine. I can't very well continue as I am.

Every now and then, some piffling wee emergency arises. Some time ago, Charlie's electrics went haywire. All her lights were flashing: her flat resembled a Berlin discothèque. She herself looked haunted and thrown, confessed to feeling spooked and impotent. She wanted me to take charge and I did, summoning a lofty jeepish truck with orange beacons.

Our landlord was born in Bulgaria. Charlie thinks he's like a lovely little bull. Rich and smartly dressed, he's resourceful and handy, the boot of his BMW packed with expensive tools. 'My brother and I were gymnasts in our youth.' 'To make an end to everything requires a syringe full of air only.'

Have I mentioned yet the road, the prangs and skittled tots? Night and day they rumble by, the cars buses rigs refrigerated vans, Bluebird Coca-Cola Memphis Meltdown.

Which brings me to the matter of diet, healthy eating. I seem to live on chocolate-fudge muffins. I'm meant to be watching my LDL and triglycerides. I should stop smoking, begin to take a statin. I've never owned a car and walk everywhere, but I end up with angina, nonetheless.

Is the story of last Christmas worth recording? It can be told in a few brief paragraphs.

Levin. My mother, fully clothed, was sitting on the rim of the bath, her face in her hands. 'If being here with me is such a damned hardship, perhaps you'd better go.'

I flung my bits and pieces into my sports bag. I quit the house in a resolute fury.

The taxi bloke agreed to drive me south to Paekak. In the coolness of a summer evening, we motored down the island. 'The highway's quiet, the cops lying low.'

'Do they bother much with you guys?'

'Not really. We're their eyes and ears, us cabbies.'

Could he sense my shamed emptiness? Only thirty minutes ago, I'd been having dinner with my mother.

A brassy sunset oranged the world. It sounded mighty chords—soothingly. Its otherwise grave harmonics bred flaky notes of rose and chartreuse.

When last he was here, the landlord gave me a small khaki torch he'd bought at the $2 Shop.

I'm not without my fantasies. Sometimes I imagine joining a monastery, feeding chooks and pigs, imitating Christ, being of use, of use. It would have to be a monastery for non-believers, of course.

Pulling up at the stop across the road, the Big Reds screech like dinosaurs being slaughtered.

The rim of a bath is no place to sit.

Hospital

PARCELLED ENERGIES

It's a Saturday evening. Jones and his wife will soon be going out. He closes his library book and pours himself a second Scotch and soda.

Emanations permeate the home. Frilly microwaves waft through tables, chairs. Jervis too absorbs invisible streams of quanta (Jervis is the easily wounded dog).

'Snap out of it,' says Shura.

'I'm thinking neutrinos and stuff.'

'And I'm thinking stir, there's a taxi on the way.'

'Quark quark quark,' says Jones.

'You're not a bit funny. And take your feet off that.'

THAI CHICKEN

And so to the Bradshaws'. Sue and Colin live in what used to be a foundry. Their apartment consists not of rooms but shelves. These lofty platforms are sustained by wires—albeit ones as thick as bicycle spokes. Girders and bricks and gloomy voids abound.

Dinner is excellent. Concluding it, the friends linger at table. A bottle of cognac gleams; issuing from small cuboidal speakers, Vivaldi toots and chimes. 'And where are the kids these days?' Colin asks.

'Simone's at Scott Base still.' This from Shura.

'And Cory?'

'Cody's in India—or was.'

'He forgets his own kids' names.' This from Sue Bradshaw. 'More cognac, David?'

The Bradshaws tend to knock it right along. The Bradshaws have smoky histories, bohemian credentials riskily acquired. Jones however is not without credentials of his own. 'Bring it on,' he tells his hostess.

'I'm warning you,' says Shura.

'I hear you, hon,' says Jones.

Colin is rolling up some bhang. With his shaggy moustache and smudged bifocals, he looks like a certain German novelist. In fact, he directs a popular soap—not bad for a guy who once spent time in an infamous Peruvian jail.

'Come clean, Jones. Just what egregious stunts are going down in the courts *this* week?'

'I'm defending an elderly party who smothered her husband.'

'Good for you.'

'Good for *her*,' says Sue.

'For myself, I'm at war with my producer. The bitch has got it in for half my cast.'

'*Selwyn Grove*. Who needs it?'

'We do, Sue,' says Colin.

The joint has been lit. The joint is passed to Jones.

Resinously, sweetly, it pops and flares like a thatch hut afire.

'I dare you.' This from Shura.

'Watch me.' This from Jones.

CONCERTINA

Antarctica is melting. India is riven by earthquakes. Shura remains handsome, provocative, delicious. Jones feels replete with comedic resources.

Colin breaks out his squeezebox. 'I'll sing you a shanty Arlo Guthrie taught me.'

'Whatever happened to Arlo?' Shura wonders aloud.

And Colin's words are *shapes*, it seems to Jones. Fridge-sized glyphs in a range of pastel hues. 'My song concerns the good ship *Vancouver* and a young tar as sweet as a barrel of apples.'

PARTICOLOURED HEADWEAR

Shortly after two on the Sunday morning, Jones and his wife leave the Bradshaws' apartment intending to walk to a taxi rank nearby. As they're swaying arm in arm down Foundry Lane, our plot achieves a somewhat dismaying spike.

'What are you toffs doing in my alley?'

'We go where we like,' says Jones, 'at any hour.'

'You'd better give your riches over here.'

'Get lost.'

The kid limps forward orthopaedically. He brings the clean reek of strong adhesives. 'I think you should surrender up your cards. Your cards and pin numbers.'

'Here's ten bucks. Now move aside.'

The miscreant is wearing a leather coat like Rommel's, a tall woollen hat created by Dr Seuss. His sawn-off shotgun points at the ground. 'You're going to have to make . . . a less insulting offer, *hombre*.'

Shura's holding one of her stilettos. 'For two pins, my lad, I'd fetch you *such* a crack.'

'I'll handle him,' says Jones. 'I'm used to dealing with troubled types like Junior here.'

'Yeah. Right. Then handle this, you fucker.'

The gun goes off with much pneumatic force. A narrow blast of air is what Jones feels. A narrow blast of air is what destroys his shoe.

HOSPITAL

'I hopped about a bit? Before falling over?"

'You hopped. The villain fled.'

'And what did you do then?'

'I remembered my powder-blue cellphone. Summoned the appropriate services. Counselled my fretful spouse to lie where he had fallen.'

'I married a lion,' says Jones.

'You married a lioness,' says Shura.

Some tiny bones in his foot have been splintered. Morphine's icy juice tinkles through his veins. The hours pass in dreamy alienation from pain. Toward dawn, Shura goes outside to smoke a cigarette and watch the sun come up. In his wife's absence, Jones is visited by a chap in saffron robes.

The monk's head is shaven, his specs purple-lensed. 'I

hope you like barley sugars. I myself am partial to them.'

'You have the advantage, sir.'

'Forgive me. Some many years ago, you saved me from incarceration.'

'I don't remember.'

'No matter. I sensed you to be an enemy of hatred and delusion. And I think you remain a friend to the four virtues, the Palaces of Brahma.'

'Tell me, worthy one—Is it wise to believe that all actions are symbolic?'

'To shine one's shoes or drive one's car or frame one's closing argument in a spirit of prayerful optimism—This is wisdom indeed.'

'And my daughter? Safe at last? Persuaded to forsake the frozen sterility of the South Pole?'

'Even as we speak, Simone is flying home aboard an RNZAF Hercules.'

'Did you know, *arhat*, that *Ice Station Zebra* was Howard Hughes's favourite movie?'

'It kinda figures, Dave.'

Authorship

Jeep lives alone. Has given up on women. Has never appeared on television.

Jeep is a writer of cowboy books. His two published novels are *Tyler's Forge* and *Reaching Laramie*. They have never made him any real money.

Jeep keeps a scrapbook. Into his scrapbook go cuttings and tip-ins, quotations he's typed up on slips of paper. 'One has two duties—to be worried and not to be worried.' That from E.M. Forster.

10:06 a.m. Seated at his portable, Jeep tries to work. *The mare snorted. Fulgencio stood his ground. 'What brings you to these parts, Traven?'*

The killer dismounted lithely enough. 'Nothin' to fuss a yellow-bellied Injun lover.'

As slim as Shane, as dark as a cigar, Fulgencio considered . . .

Considered what? Changing his name? There were too many syllables in Fulgencio.

Problems. Always problems.

A Deep Truth Concerning Our Subject's Psyche: As a lapsed, recovering or alienated Mormon, Jeep has been trying, in and by his writing, to merit salvation and eternal life. Unconsciously, mark well.

His father thought Jeep had the makings of a fine painter. Liked his son's ability to render a perspective, hint at a distance, install a vague 'beyond' with just a quizzical tick of watery paint. 'In life, we end up doing what we do second best.' That from Marcel Proust.

11:27 a.m. Jeep rings the Ministry of Commerce. 'My picture's all to hell,' he tells the guy. 'Forget the news and *Coronation Street*.'

'Describe this interference.'

'It's sort of pinstripy. I get this horizontal, pinstripy pattern.'

'Do you have an outside aerial?'

'An inside aerial. Rabbit's ears. But near a window.' Jeep can hear the guy turning pages. Going through a manual, it sounds like. 'I say pinstripy, but . . .'

'I'm listening.'

'Corduroy. It's more like corduroy.'

That manual. Those pages. *Forms*, maybe. 'OK. Let's see. Are your neighbours having similar problems?'

'Oh deary me. Oh Lord.' Jeep is running out of battery. His Motorola has always made him nervous. This is a device bent on closing itself down. This is a gadget setting telecommunications back a century or so. And now his television is being zapped. *Crassly* zapped is how it seems to

114

Jeep. 'It really gets gross at dinnertime. At dinnertime, the real derangement starts. I'm bidding you envisage icebergs in collision, titanic fracturings of alps and glaciers, with just a hint of amoeba and ciliates—a touch of washed-out *Paisley*, if you will.'

'Floes. Protozoa. You can put them on the form.'

'I wonder how I knew there was going to be a form.'

Jeep's sales are dismal. He has never caught on with the snooty reading public. Perhaps he should clear off, head for the USA.

America has artists who specialise in deserts, camp at the edges of the deserts, paint the Mojave, Black Rock, Colorado, Gila and Great Salt Lake. Their pink-and-beige expanses, their fawn aridities. The daughter of Maxfield Parrish is one such painter. She sells her productions (acrylic on board) to boutiques in Albuquerque and Santa Fe.

The Wakeful Lover

Of Sven Tailor, this:

Slapping a padlock on his door, he descended to the street. In a narrow Formica-and-fries café, he ordered a milkshake and a toasted sandwich. Before the food could be brought to his table, he nodded off abruptly, conked out for an instant—thus upsetting the sugar bowl.

The Chinese proprietor was scandalised. 'Why you may such a fucky mess?'

'Forgive me. It's just that I haven't slept for seventy-five hours.'

Broken glass littered the streets. Sven skirted a gutted tank. In the green light of a walled cemetery, he found an interment in progress. One of the mourners was a woman he'd never seen before; like a dog recalling a distant past, a remote kindness, Sven knew her at once.

When the priest had concluded his obsequies, the woman drew Sven aside. 'I'm the one you seek. My name is Natasha.'

'Are we being watched?'

'Even now.' A beaded veil filtered her blondness. 'They sit in their car with apparatus. We must comport ourselves like fish.'

'I beg your pardon?'

'Like cold-blooded things indifferent to their spying.' She made a face of haughty, childish distaste. 'You have a weapon, no?'

'Alas.'

'Take heart, Monsieur. I will send a vehicle.'

No sooner had all the mourners dispersed than a battered Citroën arrived. Its driver was smoking a pink cigarette. 'I tike you to a plice of wurst and beer. Wurst and beer I cannot afford, myself.'

The inn was full of drunks. Many were wearing cloth caps and scarves. There were drunks supine and drunks on their knees. There were choral drunks and drunks in tears. Save once in a police canteen, Sven had never before seen inebriation on such a comprehensive scale.

His driver and guide had this to say: 'The nation's manhood? Pissed. Mike soldiers of these poltroons? Forget it.'

Chugalug, thought Sven.

Natasha received him in a room above the fray. Her black-veiled hat lay on the mounded bed beneath a simple wooden crucifix. 'My father was a very wealthy man. I was raised on an estate having grottoes and thermal springs, peacocks and giraffes. Our chapel it was wrought by Balthasar Neumann. With its forest of columns, undulating balconies and painted surfaces, it possessed a sumptuous theatricality.'

'Your confidences flatter me,' said Sven.

'Beloved of my father was his little cinema. In this he contrived to screen the films of Jean Cocteau and David Lean. Also, the James Bond pictures.'

Her meagre shoulders seemed to generate a force field of probity. And Sven himself felt hollow, vacuous—avid for her gorgeous energies. 'What must I do?' he heard himself asking.

'The regime merely teeters. It needs as many shoves as we have hands. I'm giving you this gun, an Hungarian copy of the Walther Polizei Pistole, in the sanguine hope that you will use it well.'

'You have a target in mind?'

'The Minister of Swine is a rancid little prick.'

Sven and his driver descended to the bar. A honky-tonk pianist was hard at work, his skeletal instrument quaking. 'Two brimming tankards,' Sven told the barman, 'and sausage and bread for my pal.'

The driver ate with decorum. At length, he dabbed his lips with his napkin. 'I could do with a shive,' he averred.

'Me too,' said Sven. 'Nor have I slept in seventy-nine hours.'

'How come?'

'I'm taking medication. I'm on these strangely fortifying pills, subtle but tenacious of effect.'

The driver lit a yellow cigarette. 'Pills of any kind I can't afford.'

'The lovely Natasha looks just like my sister. I'm feeling as desolate as an empty wardrobe.'

'Here's my plan. I tike you aloft in the helicopter. We look for where is best to ambush the Minister of Pigs.'

'You people have a chopper? What sort is it?'

'The gear stick protrudes from the dashboard, *that*'s the sort it is.'

'This pistol lies heavy in my pocket. I'm mournful and leaden of heart. What would we see, from above?'

'The new spaghetti junction, already reviled and discredited.'

'What else?'

'Certain wooded hills. The soft-drink plant. Small jade bodies of water.'

'Small jade bodies of water?'

'Assuredly.'

'What the hell,' said Sven. 'Let's chance our arms, Tonto.'

Full Clearance

With his nerves and splintered teeth and love of unbroken calm, Geoff has come to loathe the endless weeks of summer, when his neighbours go slightly nuts. The long hours of daylight seem to disinhibit them, lure them out of their flats and out of themselves. They become, to Geoff's horror, all too visible, all too audible. The men descend to their many paupers' cars, there to wrench and beat and play their ethnic tapes. The women grapple the hoses from the reels, sluicing their concrete landings and steps, wetting the abject lawn in the process. Iraqis and Turks, most of them. Mad to rid their thresholds of desiccated leaves, fragments of leaves.

An item appears on the book page of the paper. It describes Geoffrey Cochrane as a 'new', 'emerging' writer.

Ouch.

The year is 2001 and Geoff is 50. Has been publishing since 1976.

*

His heart has developed some weird electrical fault. In order to give it rhythmic employment, Geoff goes for long walks. He walks from Berhampore to Newtown, Courtenay Place, Thorndon. His aviator's shades are green, his pants a pale khaki. The sun has tanned his arms; the potent light of summer has nourished and fluffed up the blond hairs on his forearms. He swings along briskly, a thin man proud of his youthful figure, the grace with which he moves.

But let's not kid ourselves. His asymmetrical face is that of middle age. His mouth (how it shames him!) is a whited sepulchre. It sometimes strikes him too that his ponytail completes a picture of futility, redundancy, distance from the real. Of a Peter Pan-ish love of hovering, reluctance to touch down.

With his teeth the way they are, he has to be careful how he smiles—and at whom. But he's fond of babies and dogs; he's moved by babies and dogs.

Reports of cruelty to children preoccupy, appal me. Why are people who torture their children to death never charged with murder?

Outside the Lunchbox in upper Molesworth Street, Geoff sits at a durable, silvery table. He shuts the *Post* and puts it from him—remembering of course last Friday's glib review. A writer's life is all ambition and anxiety. Ambition and anxiety, drudgery and disappointment. And oh how very slow are the frozen wheels to turn, how glacial the schedule! So that Geoff denies himself any expectation of success, of money or honours. He stands at the end of too long a queue, a queue formed long ago while he was still drinking.

So be it. The modest dimensions of my own appointed niche are beginning to feel congenial enough.

*

Total sales of his books in the second half of 2000?

Zero.

There nonetheless arrives a friendly note from his publisher. 'Liked your director's recut of *Acetylene*. Any ideas for the cover?'

Geoff keeps the good news to himself until Saturday evening. Then he rings his cobber in Raumati. 'I dropped the shortest poems and added new material.'

'Way to go,' says Lindsay.

'Still, you know, I didn't think he'd bite.'

'Why wouldn't he?'

There's nothing on the box. Geoff dons his headphones and listens to a Peter Skellern tape. His Hanimex lamp illuminates his diary, his pouch of Drum, his Zippo lighter, his silvery-grey ballpoints. He's trying to 'imagineer', to think outside the square, to see the gorgeous cover of *Acetylene*.

And what of Lindsay? He's probably my best friend, but we seldom meet.

On the Monday morning, Geoff pops into Fish Eye Discs, finds a CD of Neil Young's *Harvest* and takes it to Seamus at the counter. 'I won't be buying this,' he explains, 'but I'd like to photocopy the artwork.'

Seamus was once Famous Seamus, a deft and witty barman in a popular bar. *'Photocopy the artwork*? You're all the same, you people. You come in here demanding . . .' But he drops the old routine and asks instead, 'You're about to commit another book?'

'I am.'

'A third salacious novel?'

'A volume of verse.'

'Good for you. I hear good things, believe me. And how did your mother like the Pope singing?'

'Her ecclesiastical Christmas box? Not a hell of a lot, from what I can gather.'

At the Starmart next door, Geoff is charged twenty-five cents for a photograph of *Harvest*. Its crisp design and exuberant calligraphy perpetuate the original record's sleeve. And speaking to Seamus has taken me back to a time when music and alcohol were all the food I needed (were food and fire, both). A couple of speakers and a Garrard turntable sufficed to finish a room. For all our promiscuity (our sexual *generosity*), we paired like birds. A nest consisted of a mattress and a paua ashtray. And when the going got tough, Judith offered to sell her not-so-precious cello. We snuck it out of her parents' house in Miramar, bringing it to the city on a bus. I remember its tine of a leg like the spike on a Prussian helmet . . . and Judith's cape and blueblack Chinese hair, her brown-as-a-coolie's legs, her firm lubricious tepid kneading grip. Judith was the one I should have secured, Judith the one I should have married, our nest a mattress and a paua ashtray.

And did I screw her up? But did I screw her up and ruin her life, or was she only in it for the sex, for Cochrane's angry cock?

The Manners Mall Postshop is a place of carpeted hush. Geoff buys a franked envelope and avails himself of a desk and a tethered pen. On the blank lower third of the photocopy, he writes a note to his publisher. 'Dear Fergus—Our design for *Acetylene* might well begin here. A further suggestion, posing as reminiscence: The old Black Sparrow bks were papery things WITH COLOURED FLYLEAVES.'

A certain amber haze. It tints the air like a subtle eclipse. Floating whitish smuts are also visible. This inoffensive pall extends as far as Newtown. A gorse fire somewhere, red and yellow and lavish?

'Makara,' the dentist tells Geoff. 'They're having to bring trucks in from the Hutt.'

'These blazes used to be an annual event.'

The Dental Department of the hospital is in the oldest part of the old brick building. In spite of which circumstance, Geoff has just had his jaw X-rayed by the CAT scan of dentistry, the IMAX camera of orthodontia. 'By crikey. I've been looking at your notes,' says Darnel, 'and I have to say it's probably time we bit the bullet on this one.'

By crikey. Who says 'By crikey' anymore? And Darnel is every inch a he, a bulky young man of average height. His eyes are black black black, as black as a vintage Brylcreem siphon. His eyes are wet and sensitive, both cordial and shy, the pupils quick to shrink to an inky stare. Spanish eyes so reactive and sexy are rare.

'You think it's time they all came out?' asks Geoff.

'Oh yeah. I'll do this one extraction now, but you're really a candidate for a full clearance.'

Geoff glimpses the syringe. Darnel lifts lip away from gum. The dentist's wrist is broad, covered in glossy black hairs, pleasantly scented. Geoff waits for the needle's spiteful sting, the push and plunge of it . . . but merely *smells* the local going in.

'Y' good?'

'I'm good. I didn't feel a thing.'

As soon as the novocaine has taken, Geoff's ancient tooth is parted from his jaw with scarcely a graunch or creak.

On the morning of the Tuesday, Gerry Melling rings. His Liverpudlian accent is not yet quite extinct. 'I've found an excuse to visit that convent in Island Bay. Do you still want to come?'

'It's the chapel I'd like to see. I used to serve mass in the chapel.'

'Far out. I'll pick you up in ten minutes.'

Gerry is an architect and poet. As the beatnik editor of a little magazine, he once published poems by a certain Charles Bukowski—but that was long ago, in Canada. With his jeans and leather jacket, his salt-and-pepper beard and round-lensed specs, he looks somewhat soulful and Russian. 'The convent itself is home to an art school these days.' (As a driver, he's snappy, assured.) 'Some of the pupils are *camped* in various rooms. Just try to look like some sort of contractor . . . and let me do the talking.'

Erskine College is a landmark, of course—an elephant-grey and many-windowed pile at the top of a steep street. According to an article Gerry himself wrote for *The Evening Post*, its style is Neo-Tudor with a leavening of 'inventive Gothic'. Corbelled chimneys are mentioned. Parapets, hood moulds and decorated gables are cited; the word 'cruciform' pops up once or twice. For Geoff, though, the convent is merely familiar, a simply coloured picture from the book of childhood. 'It's more or less as I remember it. I came up once to have a sniff about . . .'

'But weren't quite cheeky enough to go inside? Follow me,' says Gerry.

A few minutes later, the two men are moving along a nether corridor. Geoff spots the side door by which he used to enter. This is where the altar boys' scarlet cassocks were hung, and that is one of the cells the visiting priests slept in. Geoff can see a sock-strewn floor, some fat tubes of paint, a chair on which is propped an artist's portfolio. The lightbulb still hangs down on its long, inflexible flex, unaltered in its perpendicularity. At a quarter to seven of a winter morning, a priest in an army greatcoat once stood beneath that bulb reading his breviary.

A narrow flight of stairs. The room to the left at the top is no longer the greenhouse it used to be. Geoff recalls a swarthily handsome nun, a female Geronimo espoused to Jesus. And this was once a place of candles and lilies and ferns in brass pots, the odours of soil and molten wax and freshly extinguished matches. If most nuns were diabolical scolds (hysterics, in the Freudian sense), Mother Bernadine was softly spoken and kind. She dressed the altar with an enthusiast's hand, but the room that was her depot smells of nothing now.

Next comes the sacristy. The shallow drawers in which the priests' vestments lay are empty now (presumably). With his indispensable key, Gerry opens the door giving into the chancel.

The altar looks less *grand* than once it did—less tall, less white, less ornate. Almost forty years have passed since Geoff last saw it. The red-lensed lamp warning of Christ's incarnate presence has been doused and removed. The tabernacle is void, deconsecrate. And where is the burnished gong I'd tap as the host was elevated? And when one loses one's faith, what is lost and what replaces it? How *much* is lost—and what replaces it?

'It's all as you remember it?' asks Gerry.

'Pretty much. The whiteness seems a little abated. What sort of stone is this?'

'I'll check the specs when I get back to my office. The chapel as a whole is Alsacian Baptismal in form and layout. It's marred by the adjunctive stuff, alas.'

Geoff continues to stand before the altar. 'Hard to credit, perhaps, but I stopped believing on this very spot.'

'How come?'

'Tricky to explain. Various forces converged and collided. Puberty arrived, certain temptations started to beset me. The upshot was, I began to take Communion sacrilegiously.'

'Sounds naughty.'

'To receive the Eucharist in an unshriven state? The blackest sin in the book. Only a few years later, I read all about myself in James Joyce's *Portrait*.'

'I've *read* the book, of course.'

'"Ever to be in hell, never to be in heaven . . ."' Geoff turns to Gerry. 'You were born in Liverpool. Does that mean you were brought up a Catholic?'

Gerry looks abashed. 'A half-arsed Anglican, me. Not really even that.'

Takes

#1

—What are they doing now?
    —They've gone to the van for some duct tape.
    —Duck tape?
    —Duct tape.

#2

—Do they have gin in the van?
    —I shouldn't think so.
    —Port?
    —I shouldn't think so, no.

#3

—We're here tonight in conversation with . . .
    —May I wear my Polaroids?
    —We'd rather you didn't, rather.
    —It's just that the glare off that reflector thingy . . .
    —We push it any further we're up against . . .

—You're up against the tubs and taps and so forth.
—We're up against the tubs and taps and so forth.

#4

—We're here tonight in conversation with ... the redoubtable Nancy Thring, a woman the *LRB* has called ... well, *what* have they called you, Nancy?

—I think their term was Ancient Martianess.

—And what was your reaction to that ... that *characterisation*?

—Oh, you know. Hyperbole, you know.

(*Somewhere OFF, a very loud heliotrope phut.*) —Ah. We seem to have lost ...

—Never mind. Could I have a smidgen more ginger ale?

#5

Audio only.

The CONSERVATORY is in darkness. Also, it's full of botanical entities which complicate the electrician's task. A brass band can be heard rehearsing in the nearby Masonic Hall.

—Do you dream, Mister Interviewer?

—Sure.

—I had a dream the other night.

—Uh huh.

—A woman I once knew ... A woman I once loved ...

—Soon have the lights back on.

—I was watching her sleep. She was sleeping very soundly. Hers were all the lineaments of beauty and

129

innocence. Later in the dream—you know how things turn poisonous in dreams—I heard that she'd been charged with shoplifting.

—How very unfortunate.

—It was only a dream, Mister Interviewer.

—Nigel. My name is Nigel.

#6

Audio only.

screeeeeeeeeeeeeeeeeeeeeeeeeeeeeeeeeeeeeeeeeeeeeeeee

—Tell a dream and lose a reader. Henry James said that.

#7

—We're here tonight in conversation with a woman whose work has been likened to that of Kate Wilhelm. Let's turn the clock back Nancy to a time . . . when you travelled to work on a tram and wrote your first reviews on an Underwood.

—A Remington, in fact. We didn't have these modern chaff-cutters. Reviewing was my bread and butter then.

—Tell us about that.

—In any given week I'd find myself reading a liquorice-allsorts mix of Romance, Adventure, Scientifiction . . .

—Scientifiction?

—Science Fiction in its adolescence. Typical of the genre was Hugo Gernsback's *Ralph 124C41+*, originally serialised in *Modern Electrics*.

—Now we're getting somewhere.

—Ever hear of Olaf Stapledon? Mathew Phipps Shiel? Lucian of Samosata?

—It isn't often my notes . . . come up empty, like.

—The Fifties ushered in luminaries like Heinlein and Asimov, *The Green Hills of Earth* and *The Caves of Steel.* And then one day I thought you know by God, *I* could write this crap!

—You don't mean *crap*, of course.

—Don't I? You know what Nige, I gotta powder my nose.

#8

—By way of resumption, Nancy . . .

—By way of resumption, yes . . .

—I'm wondering tonight . . . *which* of your hundred and twenty-seven novels . . . you regard with the least dissatisfaction.

—I've always had a soft spot for *Crystal Circuit. Transparent Cities* too had something I . . .

At this point in the taping, a bain-marie is wheeled into the CONSERVATORY. The curry has been made with Namjai Curry Paste. The Bombay duck contains no duck at all. Also on offer are seedless mandarins and after-dinner mints.

—Splendid! Champagne at last, Nigel! *(Nancy dons her Polaroids, raises her glass of bubbly.)*

—I give up. *(The CONSERVATORY is thronged by plants both monstrous and sapient—Triffids, probably. That they have somehow mediated his defeat, NIGEL doesn't doubt. He puts on his own groovy shades, a pair of Dirty Dogs.)*

—I'm old. I dream of death. *(NANCY'S tone is one of*

rueful gaiety.) I dream of lovely women I have known . . . and I dream of being dead. In death I'm flying in my son's seaplane across a gently undulating desert. It's very quiet and peaceful, there in the company of my adult son, in the cockpit of his old-fashioned seaplane. The desert below us is pink, as finely wrinkled as skin immersed too long in water—the skin of a finger, for instance.

—What can I say, Nancy?

—Say nothing. And fetch me a Corona.

screeeeeeeeeeeeeeeeeeeeeeeeeeeeeeeeeeeeeeeeeeeeeeeeeeeeeeeeeee

Before sound is lost altogether, the brass band in the distance attempts an air by Erik Satie. Gymnastic bloody pedalling *thinks NIGE.*

3

WHITE NIGHTS

It is the peculiar power of mirrors to show us what is not there.
E.L. Doctorow

WHITE NIGHTS

Passion-fruit

This particular city was a place of zigzags, trolley buses and neo-Gothic churches.

The taxis were clean and new, but for a time there lingered chalky-walled old picture theatres whose curtains of faded green velvet creaked and rattled when raised.

The Topaz. The Topkapi. Screening on dismal Sundays, *Psycho* and *Dr Strangelove*. Smoking *de rigueur* in stalls and dress circle.

Bibulous and jadedly 'showbiz', the ageing projectionists manned ginger projection booths. Eschewed ties and often neglected to shave. Traipsed home at midnight (those dank zigzags again) to suppers of toast and sardines.

Doing smack in a basement, Ajax Jones.

Jill Bradford's crowd frequented the Tutti Frutti, a milk bar of mock-rococo charm. Its pink-wafered sundaes came in hefty cut-glass boats, its foaming spiders in thick-stemmed goblets.

Neville was more of a fixture than a feature. His nickel

plating had worn off in places, revealing the plumbeous alloy beneath. A robot of the historical ZXJ type, he cleared and wiped the counter and the tables—in pathetic fits and starts.

Jill had her eye on a babe. Long legs and narrow hips. There he was at the far end of the counter, holding a can of creaming soda and looking woefully cute.

'Do you happen to know his name?' Jill asked the robot.

'Indeed I do, Miss Bradford. Got quite a lunch on him, ain't he?'

'What can you mean, Neville?'

'Beggin' your pardon, ma'am, but that young man up yonder is Luke Raven, the painter and musician.'

A good night's work behind them, Ajax Jones and Fat Johnson. They'd just knocked off a pharmacy. Come away with many a pretty capsule, tablet, pill.

'Listen up, Ajax.'

'Give it a rest, Fat Johnson.'

'A basement like this, you want to do it out.'

Ajax Jones affronted. 'How do you mean, do it out?'

'Listen to Fat Johnson. With a can of black paint and a red lightbulb, you've got yourself a strip joint.'

Luke Raven's Levis concertinaed blackly above his ankles, just as in their designer's facile sketches. As gorgeous and undead as a famous suicide, he looked like a version of Hamlet. The troubled Dane of Victorian daguerreotype, all kohled eyes and feathery Roman haircut. He probably dyed his hair that jetty jet, but his sad angelic face seemed wholesomely authentic.

Jill went to the Ladies out the back, contriving to seem to spot him as she returned. 'Hi,' she said. 'What gives?'

'Logic, grammar and rhetoric. You know these terms?'

'They're not entirely unfamiliar.'

'They constituted the trivium of medieval scholarship. A trivium being also a place where three roads met.'

'And you know this how?' asked Jill.

'Neville told me. He dithers and farts about, but he knows his stuff.'

'I dither and fart about, but I still have an excellent mind,' the robot warbled.

'What you have is a *brain*, whatever its condition.'

'I stand corrected, sir. Ain't no flies on you, Mister Raven.'

This particular city was a place of zigzags, trolley buses and neo-Gothic churches.

The YMCA offered cheap rooms. A lofty viaduct attracted the despairing.

Slung above intersections, slack but sturdy nets, the wires and cables of the trolley-bus system. Sketchy webs suggesting the hit-or-miss knitting of mescaline-fed spiders.

You could however do yourself a favour. Before you joined a choir or Scrabble club. Before you joined a choir or Scrabble club, you could check out the torrid Tutti Frutti. Amid the mirrors and 'onyx' pillars of which . . .

'So what do you put in your paintings?' Jill was asking Luke.

'Diesel locomotives. The Pie Kart in rain.'

'Cool.'

'No. But listen. My paintings are made of gouts of oil

137

and blood. Gouts of oil and semen.'

'Way to go, I guess.'

'No. But hear me out. My studio used to be a warehouse. I live with the sounds of trucks and trains and forklifts. I live with a melancholy, edge-of-the-city vibe.'

'Like who dumped the mattress in the fennel?'

'Like, *Who dumped the mattress in the fennel?* Exactly.'

And Jill had long since glimpsed. And Jill had long since spotted the bulge in Luke's black jeans, the rubbery-looking bulb of his glans. 'Gouts of blood and oil, eh? So when do I get to see your studio?'

Luke Raven shrugged. 'What are you doing when this place closes?'

Neville came to life. The Walter Brennan of robotics stirred. 'He doesn't have a kitchen. He'll feed you jumbo hot dogs from the Pie Kart.'

'I'm counting on it,' Jill Bradford said.

Greg Becker

His TV cracks and bangs as it cools down after an evening's viewing. Crisp reports as loud as pistol shots. But why does he never recall this unpleasant fact of life until his head hits the pillow?

They startle and bore him, both, these resonant detonations. He should never have moved the Sony into his bedroom, but this is where he gets the clearest picture—which isn't saying much.

Marvellous colours tonight, but only because it rained, bucketed down for most of the evening. His reception comes right with a vengeance whenever it pours. And he watches television for its colours, the brilliance of its hues. Its witch's oils, its Japanese-tartan dyes.

Or so he tells himself. And when at last he gets to sleep, he dreams. Dreams of a girl he knew some thirty years ago. She's pregnant now, her belly roundly packed, her belly tautly round and somewhat mottled, and he knows he's the father of her child before she says a word.

*

Greg Becker works in what he suspects is really a sheltered workshop. His hours are few and fluid, his tasks uncomplicated; he's given jobs unlikely to vex and derange him. And Greg has his own tidy bench, his own modest arsenal of tools. He rehabilitates toasters; he disassembles heaters and gives them the treatment, restoring them to glowing states of grace. The innards of your iron need a blob or two of solder? Greg is not unmanned by the pricky guts of things. Those luscious-looking wires of brown and green and yellow, of palest turquoise and rosiest cerise— they soothe and settle Greg, they hold him in the moment.

His therapist trained in Melbourne, Australia. Her name is Helene Wong, and she goes in for doctorly white coats. What did you see on your way to my office, Greg?

I saw the usual fountains. I saw the usual palaces, piazzas.

What else?

The sky, of course. The sky seemed kind of leaden.

The sky looked leaden to you?

All right. Point taken. I'm turning to lead myself is how I feel.

Television. Work.

Helene wears spectacles with pinkish frames. You feel any better today? she asks.

A little. Not much.

You don't think the implant has helped?

Not much. Not really.

Give me a number, Greg.

140

On a scale of one to ten, I'm feeling sort of three-ish.
Ah ha.
Three-ish. That's it. That's me.
Ah ha. OK. But we have some options here.
We talk to the techies again?
We talk to the technicians. We boost the amplitude
would be my guess.

A wingèd lion. A saint on a crocodile. And this is a city in
which . . . Canaletto meets Saatchi and Saatchi.

So let's get this straight.
    Let's.
    You were one of the guys who walked on the moon?
    I was.
    You were trained by NASA? You wore the special suit?
    Copy that, Houston. I'm the guy you never heard about.
I walked on the moon when the moon had ceased to be
news.
    Get outta here.
    It ruined my life. It blew my tiny mind.

He washes a drip-dry shirt in the sink meant for dishes.
    Greg has never emptied his suitcase, never completely
unpacked. His suitcase lies in the corner, its raised lid
revealing a jumble of socks and singlets.
    It's good to go, that suitcase. Just shut me and you're
packed, it seems to say.

A wee birdie tells me that you used to play the ukulele.
    I plinked and plunked a bit, but I couldn't make it sing.

Describe it to me, Greg.

It was cherry-red, a glossy cherry-red. It had a little Popeye stencilled in gold paint on the soundbox.

My oh my.

Exactly.

Human Voices

MAORI BILL

What year was this?

This was the year of Beirut. Beirut Beirut Beirut.

CHARLES

The Cars had a record on all the jukeboxes. *Who's gonna drive you home tonight?* it went.

Carter liked to shoot at night and in the rain, but I can't say he was difficult. And another thing. And another thing. He could drink and toke all day, mooch along all day, but when we hit the streets, alleys, zigzags . . . Instant concentration and control, wherever we were shooting.

TONY

He seemed to think in terms of tracking shots, some of which were actually doable.

We had a way with planks and bits of dunnage, and we built an actual crane out of wood. We should have been a laughing stock, but who the fuck was watching, right?

JENNY

They used a 16mm Bolex throughout.

It was real film in those days. You ran it through a clackety projector.

Real film with sprocket-holes, real film in cans.

MAORI BILL

So *Fried* is screened to thunderous applause, to wild acclaim I don't think.

So Carter's film's a scandal, an obscene provocation. A monster from the deep, a rotting heap of slime.

They're baying for our blood is Carter's take, so he rounds us up and puts us on a bus and we end up in this house he's rented on the coast. In the middle of winter, dig.

CHARLES

Sand in the bunks, the carpets. *Funeral in Berlin* and ratty old copies of *Penthouse*.

We blew some weed and ran the film again. We drew the curtains and blew some weed and looked on what we'd wrought.

MAORI BILL

Rain. Or *Night.* It should really have been called.

144

JENNY

Bernard Bliss was fabulous as Mong. And Carter had wanted that nick, that tick, that scar bisecting the eyebrow. Had wanted too of course that beautiful body.

When I saw Jude Law so gorgeously naked in *Wilde*, I thought of Bernard's pulchritude. No other word for it, kid.

CHARLES

It's actually quite a sophisticated soundtrack. Niftily layered. Craftily sculpted. If I do say so myself. And we used that Cars number to good effect.

RICHARD

He'd published a book of verse you know. I guess it'd be a collector's item now, like the poems of Ernest Hemingway.

JENNY

I fucked him and I edited his film.

Slender and nicely made. Slender and nicely made is how I'd describe Carter.

An utter bloody sod, to tell the truth. But still you know if he walked through that door over there . . .

RICHARD

I was meant to help him write the script, but he already had it in his head. And what he seemed to do was shoot a scene or two and then make a record of what he'd shot, of what he thought he'd captured. All neatly typed it was, and clipped into a binder (this biretta-black antique he'd found somewhere), and each new page was like a prose poem by Jean Cocteau.

FROM THE SCRIPT OF *FRIED*

Shot 73. Exterior. Night. The rain's very visible and wet. Neon lies in ribbons on the road. A naked MONG advances goldenly, his bobbly cock aglint like basted lamb. (There's night oil on our lens. Our clockwork consists of Brylcreem and wishbones.)

TONY

He *did* direct a picture in the States. We never saw it here, but I caught it in London in '87. Kris Kristofferson and what's-her-face. Forget it, just forget it.

JENNY

I often wish I'd seen him again before . . .

A LETTER FROM CARTER

Dear Jen,

I seem to be looking for work. Sniffing around for a project. Seeking a star (of either sort) to hitch my wagon to.

Hollywood is all I don't know what. Elsewhere, mostly. There's always 2nd-unit stuff I guess. And there's always porn, though that's a crowded field.

A working definition of Hollywood? Depravity in a tuxedo!

JENNY

They found his car parked way up in the hills.
He'd vanished. Was all we knew. For years.

MAORI BILL

Carter had come to see us before he went to America.

We had a feed and drank some beers and Carter soon
had Pania in stitches.

I was the best, he said. And I agreed.

JENNY

He'd disappeared was all we knew. They'd found his car
parked way up in the hills, keys in the ignition. And then
in '94 his remains were discovered, miles from where the
Chevy had been left.

No signs of violence. No evidence of foul play. It was
simply as if he'd gone for a long walk, walked on and on
and up and up until he'd lost himself completely to the
light, the blaze of that famous Californian sun.

White-out and deepest sleep for Carter. And when I try
to picture his remains, I'm apt to see a clean white skeleton.

UNIDENTIFIED VOICE

Who's gonna drive you home tonight? But who's gonna drive you
home? Tonight?

Alex

The Tramway Hotel is by no means full. George has a crush on one of the waiters. The young man rides a Vespa and can whistle like a guttersnipe.

George stirs his daily dose of Antabuse (a splash of greyish swill in the bottom of a glass) and drinks it with his breakfast of scrambled eggs and grapefruit juice. He sits in the sun on the terrace and opens a selection of D.H. Lawrence's poems. The book has a mosaic of tiny pink phoenixes on the cover.

The courtly old Nazi was a doctor in the SS. 'We drained the jeroboam of life. We drank deep of all that life has to offer. Down to the lees we drank, then tossed the flagon away.'

George is George Smith-Cole, the experimental novelist. He stands in the street and watches an elderly Arab artist rinsing his brushes in a fountain. Dating from 1907, the fountain resembles an elaborate Victorian cake-stand.

A lighthouse once stood on Pharos. The ancient city

boasted the Soma (mausoleum of Alexander and the Ptolemies) and the temple of Poseidon. In the time of Ptolemy II, the main library in the Alexandrian Museum held nearly 500,000 masks from the Ivory Coast, carved wooden horrors embellished with beads and cowrie shells and animal skins.

When the local barber died, several surreal collages were found in his house. In one, Bob Dylan croons *I want you* to a blonde with a Picasso tattoo.

George produces books with multiple baroque epigraphs. Some of his paragraphs are innocent of punctuation and uppercase letters; others consist of free verse. 'Literature is the orchestration of platitudes,' he writes in his mauve-leaved journal.

Mrs Prince is keen to make herself known to George. She's wearing spotless linen and a Mexican sombrero. 'Why wasn't I told you were here? *Do* come shopping with me.'

'Gladly,' says George.

When they reach her sports car, they find it covered with urchins who greet them by sounding the horn. And off she drives, darting between camels and trams and cabs and tanks, down the Rue Sultan, spinning left at the Nebi Daniel. Motor-horns compete with police whistles. Her 'little man' is enormous, bulging over a stool at his doorway, smoking a hubble-bubble. Turkish slippers of various colours and sizes dangle from strings all over the poky shop.

*

The silver-haired old Nazi won't shut up. 'Hitler himself designed our puissant flag. Our uniforms were handsome and satanic. We rolled through Europe in an ecstasy of being, our bodies young and full of the very sap of life.'

George buys a wireless and lugs it back to his suite at the hotel. When he switches the apparatus on, the horny disk of its tuning dial lights up siltily, the music of Guy Lombardo pulses forth, and George is steeped in tons of creamy tone.

The experimental novelist is smitten. Yusef rides a Vespa and can whistle like a guttersnipe. And George does a sort of slinky Egyptian shuffle, rehearsing the pouts he'll pout when he next encounters the minx.

Saturday's Paper

Ivan Quinlan no longer had a job. Flying back to Wellington from London, he'd made the final entry in his coded service diary. The life of a spy had suited him, but now it was over. On the second morning of his repatriation, he rode a bus to the armoury in Buckle Street and surrendered his weapon.

He continued however to haunt his Alma Mater, the building in Stout Street. Or did until he was challenged. 'I'm sorry, old chap, but you know the rules,' said Strong. 'Even the library is off limits to any but warranted guys.'

Quinlan went to the canteen, slipped Louise the pittance he owed her and quit the building for the last time. A beating in Brussels, a bullet in Bangkok—thus abbreviated, his story sounded trite, even risible. At only forty-nine years of age, he felt himself to be entering an inimical twilight.

Wandering through the city with his tie in his pocket, Quinlan rode escalators and glass-walled lifts. He traversed public spaces of Babylonian scale, admired gigantic saucers brimming with water.

An inimical twilight? Rather, a perilous daylight of the broadest sort.

He'd taken a room in a boarding-house in Thorndon. He swam at the local baths, explored the Botanical Gardens. And Ivan soon discovered in himself a taste for arboreal gloom. There were sodden paths with ceilings of wet fronds, smelly paths sloping down into the past; with sweat on his brow and his brain starved of blood, he glimpsed greeny steams and primitive altars.

He rang Megan Wolff from a box on Lambton Quay. She agreed to meet him for a drink or two. For six years and a bit, in the hip, hippy Wellington of the 1970s, they had been somewhat unconvincingly married; they'd also shared the lesser sacraments of hashish and Black Bombers and occasional, inhibited group sex.

A distant pianist puddled about brightly. Quinlan lit a panatella. 'So what are you up to, girl?'

'Talking books. I'm voicing talking books.'

'Do me a bit of something.'

'"Fear of the dark can be synthesised in the laboratory. Fear of the dark is an arrangement of fifteen amino acids."'

'Who dat?'

'Didion. Joan. *A Book of Common Prayer.*'

'And this you inflict on the blind?'

'It gives them a rest from Dickens.' Megan winked and popped a peanut into her mouth. 'And where are you pretending you've been for the past ten years?'

'London. Mostly London. But I worked in the film industry, buzzing all over the globe in search of locations.'

'Sounds plausible.' Her big yellow hair was as New York as ever. Nor had her figure dated at all. And Quinlan found himself remembering her breasts: though sexily vivid (or vividly sexy), they had also had a grave and dolorous aspect, had seemed to direct a sad, reproachful gaze at him.

When he touched the disturbing woman's hand, she contrived to withdraw it. 'Oops,' he said, 'I'm sorry.'

'A couple of vodkas for old times' sake—I thought that was the understanding here.'

'It was and is,' said Ivan, sober and contrite.

The following morning, he went for a swim, then drank a cup of coffee in a newly opened bagel franchise. Saturday's paper was replete with features. They told of nerve gas, the Doomsday Clock and the TB bacillus. They told of Druids and bulletproof windscreens. Ivan also read (and what the hell was this?) of restraining chairs in gas chambers for baboons.

Returning to his boarding-house, he was met by his landlady. 'Shall I take your towel and togs and hang them out?'

'Thank you, Mrs Sloane.'

The bookcase in the hall was crammed with condensed books and boxed jigsaw puzzles. Parking his thin cigar in a small, triangular, baize-bottomed ashtray, Ivan rang Megan for the second time in a decade. 'I never really got over you,' he told her answering machine. 'I sweated blood and wrestled fucking angels, but I never really got over you.'

Dak

Zane is doing the driving. He fancies himself as an expert, an adept. His hands are brown with greenish veins and he drives with a certain floaty insolence. He's wearing a yellow baseball cap and shades with bronze lenses. When the highway passes through some pissy half-arsed town, he slows, then slows some more. 'Why're we stopping?' Dak asks. 'We were always going to have to stop somewhere,' Zane answers. So Dak grabs up the pistol from the floor while Zane parks with cocky sly aplomb on the hot gravelly whatsit, the shoulder, and the two men leave the car and saunter back to the soiled mustard hutch of the tyres-and-petrol place.

The swoony slow-mo whiteout of noon. When Zane and Dak return to the Holden, they're in no more hurry than when they left it. 'It got outta hand,' says Zane. 'No it didn't,' says Dak. 'There's gunk on your shirt. Matter.' 'I shot him in the face. You shoot them in the face, you end up with matter.'

They burn a little rubber taking off, a bad-boy flourish Zane can't resist supplying. Dak returns the Webley to the

154

floor, then counts the money, the 'takings'. 'Three hundred bucks we scored,' he announces. 'It'll keep us moving,' says Zane. 'Yeah.' 'It'll keep us moving.' 'Yes.' The landscape they're driving through is flat, with fences dividing the brown from the gold, the gold from the brown. The crude hardy crippled little trees have all been bent in the same direction, smeared over by the wind. 'It's hot in here,' says Dak. 'So crack a window,' says Zane. 'Like I haven't already, penis head.' 'So shut the fuck up and light me a smoke.'

They stop to succour a babe, a hitchhiker. She's very fine indeed in her hippy cowgirl jeans, her halter and caramel midriff, and she wants to sit up front, be one of the boys. 'Where to?' asks Dak. 'I'll tell you when we get there.' 'Got a name?' 'You can call me Tess.' 'I'm Dak and this here's Zane. We've been inside for many moons. You want to do us both?' 'Sure.'

She plucks the cigarette from Zane's lips. Puts it between her own but doesn't inhale. And the country, the countryside slides by, as drab and had-it as an old khaki whatsit, an old army quilt if there is such a thing, if there ever existed such an item. The blue sterile sky is somehow cooking the land, and Dak could do with a Coke, a lemonade. Says Zane, 'I know a guy who runs a motor camp, it's handy to the beach et cetera blah blah, we could park up for a bit and do the business.' 'Forget it,' says Dak.

A cop car's belting toward them from up ahead. Its siren mute but its beacons spinning palely, it wallops by *phliBUSH* with tremendous rocketing force.

Dak says nothing. Zane says nothing. 'Did you ever wonder why humans don't eat horses?' Tess asks.

Russians eat horses thinks Dak. Russians and Mongolians perhaps.

The babe continues to follow her train of thought. 'I'd like to go to one of those old-fashioned tearooms? Where the tables have those gingham tablecloths and they serve you scones with jam and whipped cream? And maybe there's a field just right next door, a paddock with a nice old whitey horse you can feed carrots to?'

Include me out thinks Dak. Time's a fiery torrent and there's matter on my shirt. It's only castles burning but there's matter on my cheek.

Webley and Scott, Birmingham. Zane's hands are brown with greenish veins. And the futuristic city's coming up, is visible already as a watery mirage, a wobbly liquid vision of skinny towers and lofty viaducts, of aquariums and operating theatres, of helicopters and rogue shopping trolleys, of Bristol Freighters and silent eyes and peach-coloured cellphones. We'll be docking soon thinks Dak.

Drink turpentine. Buy money. Mortise & Tenon will make your dream wardrobe a reality.

Ecuador

'The river's looking pretty again today.'

'Crimson. A crimson river.'

'The paint factory's doing crimson today.'

'Yesterday, chrome yellow.'

'Tomorrow, Day-Glo orange.'

'Still and all I'm buzzled.'

'You're buzzled?'

'I've got a headcold. Forgive me. But I'm buzzled as to why we never see black.'

'Black? Perhaps they do their black in the dead of night.'

'Thad'll be it. I dare say thad's the reason.'

'You can stop being buzzled.'

'I can stob being buzzled, on thad score ad least. And turn my thoughts to other, related gwestions.'

'Other, related gwestions?'

'Indeed. Such as why there isn't a law.'

'Laws abound. There's any number of statutes. There are regulations, codes, enactments and ordinances.'

'Bud the paint sods ignore the bloody lod?'

'Their contempt for the courts is as gaudy as the river.'

'It's the frogs I feel sorry for.'
'The frogs and the ducks. The riparian denizens.'
'The riparian denizens, both gread and small.'

'Are you taking anything? For that nasty cold of yours?'
    'Hondey and aspirind.'
    'Aspirind and hondey?'
    'Don't mimic and mock. I'm dying here.'
    'Would you like a sandwich?'
    'What sord?'
    'Fish paste. I think.'

'There's that dog again.'
    'Just look ad the ribs ond him.'
    'Here, boy! Here, Devil!'
    'You know ids name already?'
    'Not really. It probably hasn't got one.'
    'Probably nod.'
    'It's just another brown, anonymous hound, half starved and homeless.'
    'It liked that bid of sandwich.'
    'Good dog! Good Devil!'

'Have you been to the post office?'
    'Nod today.'
    'You're not expecting a letter or a cheque?'
    'I've quide abandoned any hobe of either.'
    'Me too.'
    'I wander through the picturesque ruins. I go to the museum and gaze ad the objecds. I ead my meagre subber of pilchards and sago . . .'

'And wonder what might have been?'

'And wonder what mighd have been. Exacdly.'

'And you seldom open a newspaper?'

'Crossword buzzles were once a hobby of mind. I sid in the blaza and regred the poverdy of my Spanish. Am I misting anythink in the way of nudes?'

'News? *The Picayune* is full of it. Plundering Peru and Mexico, the conquistadores have come and gone. More recently, the Pope has endorsed the cult of the 17th-century "flying monk", Saint Joseph of Copertino.'

'Thad lasd's a name on everyone's libs, for sure.'

'A simple-minded Franciscan friar, was Joseph. But he stunned congregations by levitating and flying. Witnesses record that after falling into a trance, he would utter a loud cry and rise into the air, sometimes gliding out of the churches in which he preached and across the hills for several kilometres.'

'Way do go, Joe!'

'Put on trial by the Inquisition, Joseph flew over the heads of his interrogators, causing them to refer the case directly to Pope Urban VIII. Who was himself astonished by one of the monk's ecstatic flights.'

'You're making this ub, of course.'

'I'm not. Joseph of Copertino was canonised in 1767. He's the patron saint of aviators and students.'

'Why studends?'

Coffee

'*Bonjour* and good morning,' Penny says.

The hotelier has armed himself again. His shoulder holster resembles a soiled athletic support. 'All impending mail has been retarded. I hope you are not expecting missives.'

'Not so much as a postcard,' Penny fibs.

A weird mustard shadow fouls the square. Plantain and palm look darkly vital, luscious. Not to be deterred by the imminence of deluge, Penny sticks to her usual routine.

A ten-minute walk gets her to the airport. Where she sits on a single cappuccino, not entirely feigning to read a year-old *Newsweek*.

Two idle snitches eye her up, clocking her presence here in the Schooner Lounge. The younger one is wearing 'Gucci' shades, the fakey chic of which he's still getting used to. Or so it seems to Penny.

She tries to light a Chesterfield. How sick one gets of the island and all its bad actors! Even the local matches are shoddy. Explosive, sulphurous. Apt to fuse themselves with the striker on the box.

'Allow me,' says the cop, extending a biscuit-thin lighter.

'Thank you.'

'It is one of my functions, no? Seeing to the comfort of peeved and frazzled tourists?'

His face is somewhere between the Chinese and the Mexican. It's not a face to inspire inordinate dread. 'I'm much obliged, *monsieur*,' Penny purrs, 'but you seem to have the advantage.'

'Forgive me. I'm Lucien Kimbali, Chief of Police.'

She offers him her hand. 'Penelope Ashton. An American citizen. My passport's in the safe at my hotel.'

'Ah but of course. I have seen it for myself. And your picture it fails to do you justice.'

Her hand has not been shaken. She withdraws it. 'Am I in some sort of trouble?'

A brief moue. A shrug. *'Mais non*, my dear Miss Ashton.' In his uniform of gold and olive green, Kimbali looks like a glorified zoo keeper. He smells, however, richly floral, fruity—like a gust of fragrances from a jellybean factory. 'The body in the swimming-pool, the car bomb outside the consulate, the hand grenades and Kalashnikovs found on the waterfront—what can you possibly know of these?'

'Nothing whatsoever,' Penny says.

'I hope not. Devoutly. But allow me please to sit with you a minute. Do you like my aftershave?'

'My olfactory acuity is poor.'

'I smell like a vat of mashed pineapples. As we're both quite uncomfortably aware. Suffice it to say that my wife is not sufficiently wary of the native merchants.'

Penny holds her tongue.

Kimbali produces a yellow cardboard wallet: photographs.

'The body found in the swimming pool was that of a forty-year-old CIA operative. You talked to him at length at Doctor Sutton's garden party. Am I ringing any bells, my subtle Miss America?'

Fade-out

I'm ambushed by a mob of tattooed yobs. I'm making for the sea when I'm confronted. I'm in a dank, low-ceilinged, rough-hewn sort of tunnel leading to the harbour when the louts decide they owe it to themselves to fuck with me and mess me up somewhat. They punch their palms and make lascivious faces, but then it emerges that *I'm popular with them* . . .

hOW CAn i FIND SCa

Where is Scanlon? How can I find Scanlon, lost as I am in the vast, humid, overcast city he calls his own? How can I telephone Scanlon if I don't know his number?

Do I have an abode? A room in a hotel? Luggage? Have I left a suitcase perhaps in some motel somewhere? Have I ever had a home, of any sort?

A foxy female publicist shows up. 'You're scheduled to appear at Giordano's this evening. I trust you've got your own copy of the book?'

'I'm not sure I have.'

'Never mind. Plenty at the venue. I've gone that extra mile on your behalf, but you're very big already in this part of the world.'

'Big? Already? Me?'

'Giordano's seats ninety. I introduce you, you read from *Petroleum Jelly*, we take requests and questions for ten minutes, tops.'

'And then you break it up?'

'And then I break it up and the HarperCollins broad presents you with your prize money.'

'There's a light above the lectern?'

'Hey. Don't worry about a thing. I'm sure you'll be sensational.'

She zooms off in her cherry-red sports car. The quarter in which she's left me has a sticky, corrupt, New Orleansy feel. Masses of vegetation drip from balconies with wrought-iron balustrades.

I'm taken up by a gent in a white panama. 'You could do with a suit, laddie. I've a nice fawny suit you can have.'

The man bears a strong resemblance to Scanlon. Am I entirely sure he *isn't* Scanlon? 'I'm really not in need of a suit,' I tell him.

'No? Hemingway eschewed underpants. Disliked underpants but had a fondness for guns. And didn't he at some stage commandeer a tank?'

'Probably.'

'I tasted combat myself, in Pharaoh's army.' White Panama looks spookily distant. 'When dawn came and the fog began to lift, we could see what he was up to. Warpaint black pyjamas monkey wrench, a deucedly unnerving spectacle. He was doing his best to take out our auxiliary, we let him have it pop kerwhiffle plop, we disappeared him good the crazy slope. Turned him into a soup of bloodied water and chopped parsley may God forgive us. Never found the wrench, it's still in orbit I guess, up there with his kayak and his telescopic blowpipe.'

Cut to a colourful bar. We seem to be drinking in a bar, White Panama and I.

Do I have money? How much do I have and where do I keep it? Am I broke again, completely, as I always was as a young man? How am I to pay for the bourbon and Coke in my hand, and *should I be ingesting alcohol at all*, given my many past failures and despairs, despairs and failures?

Dissolve to a muggy grey elsewhere. I wander, in a floaty sort of way. I ooze or tend miasmally in this direction and that. But here it is at last, erected all about me in a twinkling, the floor and walls and ceiling of Penelope's People, the most prestigious agency in town. And the woman of the cherry-red sports car has multiplied, has become a team, a chorus of publicists. 'You're a breaking story, man.' 'You'll never guess who I've got on the line!' 'Do you fancy a gig in Berlin?' 'Would you like to appear on Letterman?'

Letterman. Parkinson, Oprah. 'But I don't want it,' I find myself saying. 'It's all too silly for words and I don't want any of it.'

'Sure you don't.'

'A little goes a long way. I preferred obscurity.'

'But you'll do Giordano's?'

'I'll read at Giordano's, if I can find it.'

'Then you'd better move your butt. You're on in an hour.'

Very well. So be it. And thus I embark on what begins as a scramble (the streets are suddenly full of rush-hour traffic), but ends in the sadness of desultory traipsing (I can't find a taxi, yellow or otherwise).

No, I can't find a cab and I can't find Giordano's. The broad wet avenues are emptying; lights are coming on in the tall apartment buildings; my last chance to live is dwindling, dwindling.

Where will I sleep tonight? But where will I bed down, tonight and in the future?

Perps

1

On planet JXZ-19, the liquorice logs are delicious, particularly those with apricot centres.

No inhabitant of JXZ-19 enjoys being idle. Many like to fashion leather belts, stamping them with dies and staining them with inks of green and red.

4D takes K8 to a drive-in movie. K8 notices that 4D has secured the top button of his shirt. 'What, you queer or something? No self-respecting guy on ZXJ-19 ever does up his top button.'

'I've got a hairy throat,' says 4D.

'But I like a little hair on a man,' says K8.

'There's an ape inside me, trying to grow his way out.'

Tangerine moons supply a nice effulgence. The movie, however, is nowhere. 'This picture stinks,' says K8.

'How's about fellating me, sweetheart?'

'Only if you've remembered to bring the peppermint mouthwash.'

'Drat,' says 4D. 'Tarnation.'

2

At another time, in another part of the cosmos, René Lalique and François Coty are having a yarn on the dog-and-bone.

'Good of you to ring me, François.'

'Not at all, my dear René. Listen. I've invented an entirely new perfume.'

'Good for you, François.'

'A brave new fragrance which must go to meet its public in bottles by Lalique.'

'Well bethought, my friend.'

'The world embraces your frosted surfaces, your inlaid colours and deep-relief designs.'

'It does indeed, François.'

A crackle on the line, as of summer lightning. 'Are you still there, René?'

'Of course.'

'Ah. I still get rather nervy, using the telephone.'

'No need for that, you silly sausage you.'

'Yes. Well. Just because the great Lalique continues to escape electrocution . . .'

'Not so his portly maid, alas.'

'What was that? Hello? You seem to be breaking up, René.'

3

Worry and inaction beget one another. Worry and inaction demand discussion. If not here, elsewhere. If not now, soon.

4

'Your tales are short and slight, Mr Lee.'

'Just so.'

'Short and slight, but lovely.'

'Thank you. It amuses me to write them.'

The interviewer presents the elderly Chinese with a bottle of ouzo wrapped in Christmas paper. 'You seem to own but few books, Mr Lee.'

'Five. And they suffice.'

5

'Where you bin, Stevie?'

Detective Steve Targett frowns. 'Minimart. Bought a can of beetroot. Did I miss much?'

'Not a goddamn thing. Perp throwed a goddamn fit is all.'

'Inconsiderate freak. And you did what?'

'Adopted a hands-off, wait-and-see profile.'

'You did good, detective.'

'Perp'll maybe need his tongue sewed up.'

'Scant blemish there, attaching to ourselves.'

'High-strung goddamn perps. They can't stand the heat, they should get out of the kitchen.'

'Amen to that, Ricardo.'

It's four in the afternoon. The water in the cooler's lukewarm again. Ricardo's wife of three weeks swings by.

Wild spiders crying, thinks Steve Targett.

Buying beetroot was a mistake. Whatever elusive nutrients my body and soul are lacking, beetroot tinned in Mexico will never supply them.

Worry and inaction. I've fallen for a twenty-three-year-old crackhead. I pick him up on Sunset Boulevard, I buy him burgers and cigarettes, I offer to pay to have his teeth fixed, but he'll only see me Tuesday afternoons. I'm not quite real to him, he thinks I come from a distant planet, he can't quite find me likely, credible.

Worry. And inaction. And wild spiders crying.

Cactus Juice

1ST DISK

Rick Gadd had washed and dressed. Yip Nash was still in his cot.

Molloy entered the cell. 'You guys are really getting up my nose.'

'Good morning, Occifer.'

'I've had it with your crap.' Molloy hauled all the bedding off Yip, dumping it on the floor. 'I want you up by the time I reach this slot. And you, Gadd—you'll see that he complies.'

'I'll try, Mister Molloy,' Rick told the departing screw.

The gaol was all moist ramps and passages. It smelled like a grandstand in winter. When you spoke above a whisper, your voice slapped the walls. Your voice echoed flatly, its bonky ring compacted and shaped by concrete.

Standing on his toes, Yip stretched and yawned. His body was pale but well-made and complete, chevrons of muscle above the knees.

Rick began to sharpen his 4B pencil. 'Welcome to Chelworth.'

'What did we do to deserve that wanker?'

Rick tapped frilly shavings into an ashtray. 'He's not so fucking bad. Put on some clothes why don't you.'

The distant cities smoked. Chelworth's ashen star was itself contracting, cooling. Molloy delivered towels, spotty little apples. 'You're better off in here,' he was fond of saying. Shaped and compacted by walls, voices had a bonky ring to them.

The guys were treated to a lecture on VD, candy-coloured slides in the dark gymnasium.

Herpes. Vaginal warts. A cock with violet chancres. Using a remote, the MO shunted pictures. 'This clown was a serial infector. He carried every bug known to microbiology.'

Gonorrhoea. Syphilis. Deposits of goo hooded by a prepuce. 'That gunk you see is Cashmere Bouquet. Keep soap away from your foreskins. Under your foreskin is no place for soap.' The MO clicked his clicker. 'In this day and age, tattooing's out. And those of you with haemorrhoids should not be indulging in practices.'

They heard old news and rumours of news. Tidings sifted in like light into a cellar. Rumours came with dusk, when pigeons alighted with a clatter.

There's this one lag called Skeat. He picks up Rick's pencil and fingers it. To give him his due, he seems to respect that pencil. 'You need any smoke or alcohol, you don't want to deal with nobody but me.'

'No way,' says Yip.

'Wouldn't dream,' says Rick.

They heard the slap of wings, the soft clatter of pigeons taking flight. Caged bulbs flickered, seeming to peck. The corridors and ramps channelled sounds, the bonk and clap of voices.

Stonily white, Yip Nash stood in the shower, his sturdy legs a large part of him, water pouring from elbows and prick. His big beige knob pouted; no foreskin there.

Rick would exercise until he sweated. He did push-ups and sit-ups on the floor of the slot. He picked a flight of steps near the kitchen and ran up and down it, up and down.

A villain called Ted Smith came to the cell. An older man, notorious and gloomy, he lay on Nash's cot with his hands behind his head. 'Did you ever play golf, Yip? I liked to hide out near a golf links, take a motel unit and get in with the toffs.'

Yip sat on the floor between the cots. 'A bit of a toff yourself, by all accounts.'

'I like to think I earned a certain reputation. I was always clean and sober for a job.'

'How many'd you do, all up?'

'One too many, by the looks. I was never the dangerous thug the papers made me out. I only ever owned that silver Magnum. For good or ill, that gun became my trademark. A teller saw that piece, he knew he was involved in a quality stick-up. It made for a certain confidence on both sides, that great big gleaming mother. It was never loaded, of course, but it did the trick.'

'Would you like some gum?'

Smith took a tablet of spearmint from Yip's packet.

'They claimed you wore disguises,' said Rick.

'I distinguished myself by maintaining a makeup kit. I

173

had sticks of theatrical grease, rinses for the hair, different pairs of glasses. I could barber my hair and tint it, give my face a whole new character.'

'And yet,' said Rick, 'you always used the same silver Magnum.'

'Experts have examined the issue. What a gambler *really* wants is to lose everything.'

2ND DISK

Rick drew a pair of hands steepled in prayer.

Each morning in the slot, Yip Nash examined his shoulders for pimples. He stood there bollocky, scrunching a shoulder forward to peer at it. A nude ape fastidious and vain, he prodded and stroked each shoulder in turn.

They asked you about yourself. They asked you about the sort of kid you were, were you ever bashed or mucked about with, did you go in for torturing animals. The psychologist had spaces on a form.

'I'm not a fucking serial murderer.'

'Cool it, Rick. You're part of a sample we're following.'

Molloy delivered toilet rolls and freckled mandarins. Returning from the showers, Yip sat on his cot like a yogi, examining his soles. His long scrotum sagged; you could see the balls in it.

When Rick went to the kitchen at dawn, the pilot light on the gas range was bluely visible. Of the many dour constraints of life in Chelworth, there were those you might one day think about, isolate as having had flavour, attach nostalgia to. Autumnal things crepuscular and soothing might one day recall your time inside, remind you of a life of relative contentment.

Caged bulbs flickered, seeming to peck. Skeat went mental and wasted a screw. Rick sat a personality test, exercised till he sweated, jogged up and down his flight of steps.

The psychologist had a tan leather jacket. 'You have a problem with anger. You express your anger belatedly, in explosions of inappropriate rage.'

'So now we fucking know.'

'I'm thanking you again for your cooperation.'

'It gives me an interest.'

'Your tests show a certain conspicuous bias. You don't want to be thought effeminate.'

'There's boxes I'm not about to tick. Forget flower-arranging and needlework.'

'You completed the Minnesota Multiphasic. You're determined to evince a maximum of masculine affect. One might even infer a degree of homophobia.'

'I want to be a fireman when I grow up. I want to be a fucking test pilot.'

Rick spent an afternoon in the kitchen, skinning potatoes in the machine, freeing the big dishwasher of chips of glass and other debris. He worked in a littoral twilight, the sorrowful dusk of rainy quays.

Yip returned to the slot with a flagon of Cactus Juice. 'At last a chance to fuck our tiny brains. I scored a joint as well.'

The two-person party began after lock-in. Fixed within its strutted hutch of wire, the bulb on the ceiling seemed starved of wattage.

Yip had swished a bendy plastic cup. This he filled with the stagnant yellow mead. 'Have a go at this. It's supposed to contain laboratory alcohol.'

'Smells more like meths.'

They passed the joint between them, Gadd and Nash. The slot was soon a submarine, one in which the power was slowly failing. Yip's face looked dark and gaunt, sinister and holy. 'You lie dee Cictus Jutes?'

'It's vile fucking muck, as well you know.'

'Myself I *deeg* dee Cictus Jutes,' said Yip.

'I've been thinking more and more about absconding,' said Rick.

The joint was now a roach, a fiery speck. Yip sucked at it wetly. Trying to talk while holding his breath, he sounded like a wheezy cartoon dog. 'I've been thinking along the same lines, amigo. What say I come with you?

3RD DISK

Two screws got drunk and rioted. You could hear them larking about, kicking over the traces in C Wing. One was shouting taunts through a megaphone. You could hear the graunch and squeak of a firehose being dragged off its reel.

Boos and cheers. The sizzling gush of water. 'Mind our bedding, cunt!'

Brought to a certain level of engagement, Yip began to scowl. The gaping slit in his silvery glans became a little well. It bled or leaked a watery sort of stuff, thinner than actual come.

Ted Smith appeared again, his thumbs in his belt like an

elderly Texan cowboy. 'Mind if I linger, boys?'

'You're not looking too clever,' said Yip.

'I've asked the quack to run some tests. There are cancers of the liver and pancreas. They fan out through the body using ancient tunnels. Liver, lymph nodes, brain—that's the usual pattern of distribution.'

'We'll keep our fingers crossed,' said Rick, 'but there's something else we'd like to discuss with you.'

A Sunday night in Chelworth was a hushed, domestic time. Men turned their radios down, tidied their tidy cells, aired the socks and shirts they'd wear in the week ahead.

Rick tugged a recent drawing from his pad. It depicted a Negro in chains, and seated on the floor of a dungeon. His striped convict's jacket failed to cover his ebony chest. His extended fingers held a chunk of bread, a fragment torn from an old-fashioned loaf, and a large rat was nibbling at this morsel.

Before going to dinner, Rick Sellotaped the drawing to the wall above his cot. He quit the cell carrying nothing, not even his 4B Staedtler pencil. Leaving with nothing: he was good at that.

Sitting apart from Yip in the dining room, Rick didn't converse with his neighbours. The meal consisted of canned tomatoes and boiled saveloys. Rick dipped his buttered bread in the pink soup on his plate.

Leaving the dining room, he caught up with Yip. As they swung along together up a ramp, Rick could feel the heat coming off Yip's body. A special camera might detect the swirling aura of their intent.

Ted Smith was waiting behind a grille, his face in shadow. 'One of the lads has left the woodwork shop unlocked.'

'Nice one,' whispered Rick.

'The perimeter fence has been cut. They flagged the spot with a handkerchief.'

'Magic. Thanks a million.'

A flight of steps. A dark corridor. Once inside the shop, Rick allowed himself to start to hope. The way ahead lay through a storage cage, its door a wooden frame covered in chicken wire. Arming himself with a screwdriver, Yip began to prise bolt from architrave. And he flew at his task with savagery, tore into the job with a nasty feral greed.

Screws pinged and popped. The bolt fell to the floor. Rick entered the cage ahead of Yip, pushing a sawhorse aside and advancing on a grimy, cobwebbed window. Placed low in the slanting wall, it opened outward. Rick had to shift a bucket full of sawdust (a scuttle of thing, fire-engine red) before he could get his hand to the window's latch.

'It's free,' he hissed, 'it's giving.'

A minute later, the two men were standing on the roof of Chelworth. Rick caught a whiff of Yip, the sweaty/spermy pong of his exertions. The sun was low, the dusty light orange; wind poured through a mass of bluish pines. And Rick could see the road, the piggery, the guards' bright vehicles. What colour and pattern in the world! And it wasn't quite a case of needing wings—the drop to the turf below was one you *might* survive.

Spike Rings His Sponsor

'I got a bit of a fright the other morning.'

'—.'

'I was sitting here thinking of going to Lower Hutt. Getting on the train and going to Lower Hutt.'

'—.'

'This being something I do. This being something I do from time to time.'

'—.'

'And OK, fair enough, the last time I was in Lower Hutt, Lower Hutt sucked. A little.'

'—.'

'So I'm sitting here asking myself, *What's better than going to Lower Hutt on the train?*'

'?'

'And it suddenly came to me. And it hit me like a demolition ball. *I* know what's better than going to Lower Hutt. *I know what's better than anything!*'

'?'

'Walking into a bar with a pocket full of money—*that's* what's better than anything, that's what knocks everything else into a cocked hat.'

'—.'

'It's early in the day. The glasses yes and the bottles too are gleaming."

'—.'

'There's a hot white stripe of sunlight on the carpet. There's a numinous quiet, a sacramental hush.'

'—.'

'I'm about to mount the high white horse of booze. I'm about to mount the fleet white steed of alcohol.'

'Except of course you're not.'

'Except of course I'm not.'

'Except of course you don't.'

'Except of course I don't.'

'So tell me, Spike. Remind me. How many years have you been sober now?'

4

Little Steps

As to the house, I find it at last, much further from the station than the old one, with mountains looming behind it like things also themselves newly-acquired, drawn nearer by ownership. It is smaller than my parents' former home and has a neat, white appearance. I see that it has the advantage of being easy to paint.

I go to the back door with shyness. My mother emerges like a stranger from a fresh, a smaller kitchen.

'Oh, how lovely. *You* took your time!'

It is early evening on New Year's Eve.

Behind my mother's head a mirror is full of the pink of the setting sun. At my back is the odour of garden. A child squeals glee. I bend to my mother's cheek.

'The kids are having tea.'

In the breakfast area beyond the kitchen my sister's daughters sit at table. Ann stands above them. She seems taller. I kiss her, too, on the cheek. She is thinner of face, has achieved a definition she must previously have lacked. She is quick with odours, of the children and their foods, yes, but with all the scents of the garden as well, of leaves and their sap and of woodsmoke.

'I like your soap,' I say.

'What, good old Sunlight?'

We laugh together. I hold her at arm's-length to watch the little of myself there is in her. I see her again as a girl, see the curtsy in her look. With her I am at home, have made it to this annual celebration, to the place where the family meets.

The children have spread before them the usual holiday fare. One of the girls was a toddler when I last saw her, a little blond thing at once shy and inquisitive with bright Australian speech. Five years ago her sister had not been born. But Alice remembers something of me, my beard perhaps. She looks to her mother.

'You remember *Tony*,' coaxes Ann. The child struggles.

'I think so,' she says without pleasure, her dignity apparent. She has one of those little cheerios in her hand and will not now eat it.

'Go on,' I say with a grin. 'Have your sausage.'

'It's not a sausage,' says Alice.

'It's a sort of sausage, pet. Doesn't Anthony look handsome this year? Did you come by train?'

'By bus.'

'You would have done,' says my mother. 'The train's a thing of the past.'

Is it? I have been sober six months but am still everywhere encountering absences, of things and of people.

I take my mother in as she makes the three of us some tea.

She was once very pretty. I remember her as having been very pretty when I was a boy.

'Mum,' I sigh, 'how are you, really? I mean, how has the settling-in been? I bet leaving the old place was a wrench.'

'It was, love, it was. And sad, in a way. Jamie was here for Christmas of course and kept going to stand at the front gate, or getting into the car, you know, waiting to be taken back to the old house. He was very confused by it all, was our Jamie.'

The house of which she speaks, I know, was for her a delivery from the misery of her early marriage. My brother Jamie has Down's Syndrome. And so, yes, he might stand at the gate, any gate, and wait to be driven, or walked, back to the sombre rooms of a former, familiar existence, to the amber wallpapers of childhood's calm.

My father comes up the warm, bright street on foot. Though he does not now get any more grey, there is still something rakish in his gait, an invitation to levity that increasingly few people might recognise. His tan has made his eyes more pale, less blue. He is as familiar to me as myself.

'Hi, Dad.'

He shoots me a look of complicity from the door: I have been standing, thus, in his kitchen since last year.

'He'll get caught, yet. Your brother. He's taken the car off boozing at the lake.'

'Ah. It used to be a straight line home. How are you?'

'Good. Just fine. Apart from the piles, eh, Mum?'

'Anthony doesn't want your piles, dear. He's been waiting for some dinner.'

'Am I late? I must have got trapped at the club. Terry

had his daughter in. I said we might see them tomorrow.'

'We should be taking Jamie out.'

'Of course,' says my father. 'Are you having a beer, Tony?' he asks with a smile.

'I could go a sherry, Dad. But no, thanks,' I say. My father is silent. What I have told him must surely be news, but he is too old a bird to evince any great interest in what we will pretend is my very own business.

'There'll be no need,' says my mother. 'Ann and I would like something to eat, Alan. There's ham, pet, or mutton if you'd rather.'

Remembering past Christmases I have looked forward to something hot. Before the deaths of grandparents and the polite defections of my married siblings, Christmas and New Year were more colourful events, of sixpences and burning brandy. I take consolation in the fact that my father hates anything cold. I assemble some ham and circles of boiled egg on a piece of the Spode about which the family joke. What I need is a drink. With pity and amusement Ann joins me at the kitchen table.

'Have some pickle,' Ann jokes.

'Bloody salads.'

'Shush you yo' mouth. Bloody salads are good for you.'

'Been slaving away then, too, over a gelid refrigerator all day?'

'As a matter of fact these salads are a jolly pain to prepare. Here's poor wee Kate. Hello, darling.'

She lifts the child to her knee.

'It suits you, this motherhood,' I say.

There is a simplicity in Ann, a grace which admits this freely enough. She thrusts her jaw forward playfully.

'Yes, brother. I've enjoyed it,' she says as if of something done, somewhere visited now receding in her path. Is her marriage in trouble? I know so. My acceptance of the fact must come from without, from the evidence her changing circumstances will in time provide, signalled across an ocean.

We do the dishes, Ann and I, did them together as children. Attending here and there to her newer plants, my father circles the house with mother in the lovely dusk. I venture out myself. A sprinkler beats. The sky is slivers of peach. Inside again, I read to the children of monsters.

After their shared bath my nieces are presented to me for kissing. Alice thanks me for having kept a secret. When Ann returns from their bedroom my father clears his throat.

'Cracker kids,' he says. 'Not like you little sods were.'

Ann thinks this predictable.

'Yes. Well, there's no one around any longer to tell us what you were like at their age.'

'Much like them I would imagine,' my father says brightly. 'A drink, Mother?'

'A wine-cooler I think. And don't be so conceited, Alan. Your mother didn't think that much of you, even when you were grown up.'

We have been sitting, talking of this and that, with only the illumination a Christmas tree provides. It has gotten dark before Ben my youngest brother returns from the lake. The lights of his car brighten the lounge as he turns into the drive. He is with us almost at once.

'Evening all. Hi, Anthony. Are you staying?' I have arrived in his absence.

'Of course.'

'You can have my bed then.'

'He cannot,' says my mother. The light Ben has switched on shows her to be knitting.

'Yeah he can. I want to sleep at the Thyme Street flat.'

'I know you do. And you'll do no such thing. You'll sleep in your own bed, thank you very much.'

'I'll be all right on the floor,' I say unhelpfully.

Yo. In this I am seeming as Ben might, a cartoon figure with a haircut like a paper party hat, talking circled talk.

The women knit and talk. Ben drinks the Elephant Beer I have brought him. He affects a 'gee-whiz' amazement.

'You wanna try some of this, ole man,' he tells our father.

'You want your head read,' our father tells him.

Father plays his new Pavarotti on Ben's new stereo. He does more than hum along.

'I could have been great,' he winks, very pleased with himself and Luciano.

Midnight approaches. Ann gets Alice up. Alice dances between her mother and mine, little steps, little steps.

My watch does not agree with my father's and we turn the radio on. My mother hurries back from the kitchen. Our crossed hands reach and grasp and we have formed a circle. A drum roll begins. Then everyone is singing.

'For auld lang syne, m' dear,

For auld lang syne,
We'll tak a cup o' kindness yet
For the days of auld lang syne,'

my father's voice clear and youthful above the rest.

It moves me as it always does. And for me at least the room is crowded with ghosts, ghosts eager to be present. We who are material seem so few amidst this airy throng of others. And then we are all shaking hands or kissing and slowly, slowly, something begins to be over.

My father disconnects the Christmas-tree lights. I kiss my sister. I kiss my sister Ann goodnight.

When everyone else has gone, I settle to sleep on a lilo on the floor. The logistics of turning the light out and finding my bed again in the dark constitute my last effort of the day. I lie on my back in darkness.

I have not seen Ben in his uniform of a nurse, the inverted watch pinned to his short-sleeved smock, his fair-head's brown arms with their repertoire of strengths. I was cruel to him when he was a boy, he who has so recently become himself.

I dream of Ben. He has a present for me. It is a perfectly finished model glider, sky-blue, cloud-white, smelling of size and cement. Its wings have short, dihedral tips as if for catching at the air for height.

I am awake and up early. I make a cup of tea and take it to the back lawn. The grass is dewy, the light simple in which flowers unstick themselves from sleep. Tracing invisible geometries in the damp air, bees ferry tiny certainties about. It is here I invent the dog.

My father is shaving, the bathroom door ajar.

'I'd like to get back today, Dad.'

He dabs lather at himself.

'It's all buses nowadays,' he says. 'Inter-bloody-City, I think they call it. They travel in convoy when they move at all.'

'Where is the terminal?'

'There's a booking outfit behind the Mall. I'll drop you down there after if you like.'

Our language has been oddly sparse. I have felt it to be letting in the air like a building half-finished.

My mother, too, is up. I say: 'I have to get back today.'

A small, complete figure in a quilted dressing gown of pink, she is making tea and toast for my father.

'Never mind,' she says, perhaps to herself. 'But won't you have trouble going today?'

I will and have thought about it.

'There must be something doing. I'll ring around. I'll hitchhike if I have to.'

She looks at me squarely now (a girl with how many brothers?), her hands on her hips. There is much that is tender in her stance. Yet she wants a little more.

'There's a dog now,' I lie. 'I've got a dog now at home.'

Quest Clinic

ONE

Arriving in a van minutes earlier, Bede had felt he was about to swing down from a helicopter into this muddy notion of a place. A scale of sorts had asserted itself dimly through the rain. The building he and his driver sought had extended a discernible congruence of path and lawn toward them through a mist. Its entrance was formal enough; Bede had otherwise felt he was entering a laboratory. In aluminium letters of boxy prominence, QUEST CLINIC had announced itself.

Now, through a window, Bede could see on a bank nearby, at shoulder-height, a cow, disconsolate and halt. The sky beyond was its own grim landscape, a terrain inverted.

'It pays, you know, to have a shower,' said the man beside Bede.

Bede turned to face him. The man wore an expression suggesting he was inclined, for the present, in the present instance, to suspend the exercise of a nugatory authority. Disarmingly, behind his spectacles he had eyes which seemed not to need glasses. They were healthy enough and direct and might, indeed, have done much in other circumstances to oppress. To taunt them Bede said, 'Tonight, if there's time.'

'Oh? I thought perhaps that after the journey, the ride, the van and so on, and there's plenty of hot.'

Adjacent to the dormitory was a games room with darts, pool and a table-tennis table. Across the hall again were the showers, toilets and basins. Their whiteness was achingly cold, the purity of the place and its accoutrements doubled, it seemed, by powerful fluorescent tubes. The windows in here were of a misted, meshy kind. But cowless. And the difficulty in communal living was always to find somewhere to masturbate.

Bede's suitcase (and his low, narrow and dim new bed) were behind them somewhere now. They were passing down a watery glass corridor or passage for which Bede felt a liking. Its slope hinted at levels, at complexity. To Bede's left, dismal in the rain's wet and ragged discontinuity, walls of red brick-veneer enclosed a cute little lawn and garden. Some sort of short, monolithic statue or sculpted form peeped out through fronds with a dark, coy magic.

In the institution's lounge there emerged, at last, an architectural theme Bede thought he might live with. Here the ceiling leapt upward, a complicated arrangement of rafters and beams, of polished native timbers. There was a huge, stacked fireplace of slate, a stone, in any case, in the crystalline texture of which the spectrum seems trapped.

'Have a fire most evenings, weather like this,' said Bede's guide. 'In here you've got your kitchen. Joe does this out, keeps it tidy. Here's your tea, your coffee, all your bits and pieces. We try and keep it nice. Like a bar, really, eh?'

Bede walked the length of the room to where sliding glass doors gave a view of the valley below. There was much in this vista to interest him; Bede would save it.

It was all, today, much like a vast, indefinite tunnel with walls of a uniform puce, ruptured bluely here and there, or whitely, in which a silver opacity rolled like smoke away, away.

'Here's Greg,' said the man, and was replaced in Bede's awareness by this new one, who had at least a name, and was closer to Bede in age, though younger, with a quick, firm grip.

'Greg,' said Greg, with a squeeze, 'ward host. What do you like least about the place so far?'

TWO

Bede would recall it as having been in the evening of the day of his arrival that he was first interviewed by Dr Lardwrist. The doctor was a large man, a fat man who seemed to make a virtue of wearing very few clothes (shorts, jandals), but who set, nonetheless, a two-bar heater beaming the moment he had closed his surgery door. He smoked, too, with a relentless, a very oral fury.

'I have some notes here forwarded me by your previous physician, Heron. He mentions pancreatitis, malnutrition, asthma and . . . "a depressive anxiety state". In an ideal world, depression and anxiety would be mutually exclusive ills. Stand and open your mouth, please.'

Bede complied. Lardwrist knocked about in Bede's

mouth with a spatula. When he had finished he resumed his seat.

'You have an alcoholic's denture, all neglect and ruin, though I'll bet you haven't had toothache in years. Any clap?'

'No.'

'Excellent. You have confined yourself to bringing, and very creditably too, alone and unencumbered, yourself?'

'Yes,' replied Bede, catching on.

'Right. Well, I am here to see how I can help you. And I have a clue or two. Tell me: are you, on the whole, a happy man?'

'Yes. No. I try to be. I don't know.'

'Drink in the mornings?'

'Increasingly, yes.'

'Says here you half killed yourself.'

'A mechanical fault in the steering.'

'MOT gives you a phenomenal blood-alcohol reading.'

'I couldn't come right that day. And I remember the accident. If I'd been less jumpy I might . . .'

Lardwrist did not make notes. 'So what are you going to do?' he asked with sadness. 'With your tolerance still intact and your life all strewn behind you like so much jettisoned hope?' He paused. 'Tell me, what do you do for a living?'

'I'm a motor mechanic.'

'A good one?'

'Yes.'

'And your age?'

'Thirty-two.'

'Married?'

'I was.'

'Buying your own home?'

'She got that.'

'I see. "She got that."'

'I'm not an alcoholic.'

'No?' Lardwrist paused again. He tapped his file at last and said, 'Says here you are, in this. Your tissues say you are.' He donned a pair of wide and gleaming bifocals. And looked at Bede like an owl, like an owl looking.

Bede was in bed in the dormitory when Greg came to his cubicle.

'I've just met the quack,' said Bede. 'Is he all there?'

'Very intelligent man, our quack.'

'Yes. I have to confess I thought so.'

Greg walked away to his own bed. Bede could see him undressing.

'Put it this way,' said Greg. 'He believes in this place, believes that it works. But not for the obvious reasons. He gives a little lecture. You'll hear it. It's all awash with aldehydes and endorphins and Christ knows what, and at the end he says, "But if all this was otherwise, you'd still be alcoholics." Yeah.' He stood folding his jeans, his long thighs white and amber in the gloom. 'Cereal and toast at seven, Bede,' he said. 'You know where to go?'

'Of course. Thanks.'

'Goodnight, then.'

Earlier, Bede had unpacked and stowed his clothes, his few effects. There was a little desk on which he had disposed his shampoo, yellow radio and photograph of his daughter. He'd brought a chess-set and pieces. Perhaps Greg played. Though not every nerve in his body craved a drink, sleep would be impossible. No; what he felt was a suspension of intent. He knew, or thought he knew, that at some future time he would drink again, not moderately, in the company of friends. He saw their faces. It was as vague as that, as fatal. He knew it to be cowardly, embarking on a programme in the present with any sort of snide, secret reservation as to his conduct in the future. He could hear that the rain had stopped. He missed it. He wished it would return, interposing itself between him and the reality of his situation. He was superfluous to this place. It had no need of him. His engagement in its workings would be sterile and duplicitous. A door, a window, opened in his mind on something fragrant. He forgot his inability to weep and was soon asleep.

THREE

Bede was having breakfast when he felt his heart stop. He stood abruptly. His head felt bloodless. There was something very wrong with him. He must get to the door; he must get from the door to the lawn beyond. A great, unvital turning of the world; a bleached, recessive tilting ... The jamb of the door was like ice to his touch. His deflated, filtered consciousness made room for a feeling of panic. He had reached the lawn, but to have done so was not now enough. Like someone stunned or shot he turned. His hand encountered a face.

'Sit down. There's a bench behind you,' said a woody, cigar-box voice. 'Breathe shallowly,' it said, 'it's all a part of withdrawal.'

Through the fear and shame this fit was leaving behind, Bede became reluctantly aware of the shade in which he sat, the dewy bench beneath him and the cold, lime stripe of sunlight over which he seemed poised as if childishly constipated. There was, too, a hand on his shoulder, unpardonable but firm.

In as much of her nurse's uniform as she ever wore, Mrs Oliver came.

'Off to your groups, boys and girls. Beryl! I'll shoot you, my lady, cigarettes with your chest. Bede, dear, let's have a look.'

Like everything else belonging to this morning, Mrs Oliver's fingertips felt cool and, because Bede had shut his eyes, felt monumental on his wrist. He saw their marble prints, huge, and was briefly a child again.

'Well, my lad. I was expecting a myocardial infarction at the very least.' Who had summoned her? 'You'd best come to the surgery.'

Bede opened his eyes. From a white, marsupial pocket in her front, Mrs Oliver turned out, like something animate, a seemingly comprehensive bunch of keys: she was a repository. Bede stood. A man Bede had seen in the lounge turned, with tact, away toward a little bed of flowers. He was wearing still, or again, a plain, green dressing gown of velvet, his back and his buttocks in shadow, a wedge. And was stooping now.

'Have you thought of having roses, Mrs O?' His fingers cut at the soil, his brown thumb erect.

'They would be nice. I'd have time, I suppose. We had beauties in Christchurch, Mr Salmon, we had a lovely display.'

She took Bede by the ear and led him inside to the warmer air. Made pale by an oblique sunlight, the corridor's carpet had the pink, flat quality of something beneath water. Bede's vision was bled of lustre. He counted his heartbeats. In these present, elastic seconds the gaps in his pulse were stark, a ratchet's missing teeth magnified enormously. While Mrs O unlocked the surgery door with complacency, Bede craved swiftness.

'Have you been smoking pot?'

'No.'

'I should *think* not.'

She seemed furious with his answer. With the pressure of her fingers on his sternum, she backed him into a chair. She moulded the sleeve of rubber to his biceps (goosey, diminished) with an action Bede connected with the shaping of pastry.

'It's just that if you're feeling anxious,' she said, and began to pump the spig's pneumatic bulb with vigour, 'any agent of that sort . . .'

'Ouch.'

'Sook. Well, that's OK if a little low for your age. No. If you're a little jumpy, pot is *not* the thing to be . . . My God, the time. *Where's* that silly doctor?'

As Bede's thermometer cooked, Mrs O rattled away at the telephone keys with a look of professional cunning.

'David?'

'—.'

'I thought I'd find you there, yes. Look. It's the Ford boy. I don't think he's quite over the hill yet, an episode this morning . . . Cardiac neurosis . . . Sweating . . . Frenetic . . . What do you mean? David! I asked that man to drop it where it's always dropped. Fool. Did she? How queer.'

Mrs O hung up with a chastened look.

'We're putting you on a sedative for a while. These things happen'—she took the thermometer from Bede's mouth—'when the system reminds itself of the presence of alcohol in the tissues. Its release from the marrow can take up to two years.'

'So now I know.'

'So now you know.'

They stood and she hugged him. It was a measure, he supposed, of the very nether ebb at which the needle of his confidence seemed to be stuck that he should guess possible for an instant . . . But no: Mrs O was old enough to be his mother.

FOUR

Sometimes the lounge had its curtains drawn. Before Bede could finish his tea and return his cup to the servery, a fleshy motion-picture might animate the wall, its soundtrack booming, of brusque and limited people quarrelling or water-skiing or tossing drinks down sinks, in green or ochre fluxes of the light. Bede knew himself to be doped. Gatherings took place. Now in the lounge, now in a comfortable room in which someone absent seemed otherwise to live, groups of patients cohered with the apparent purpose of discussing travel. Bede seemed to himself to belong, obscurely, to one such group. It formed around him once, in a workshop he had discovered, while he cut from some colourful felt the components of a parrot he thought he might make for his daughter. In time, his medication was withdrawn. Bede at last discerned, between breakfast and bedtime, a ladder of more or less formal obligations.

In truth, Quest Clinic followed a schedule, a programme of therapies sometimes extending into the evening. When Bede's initial illness ended he found much of what went on in the place of interest. But group therapy he loathed. One morning a new arrival joined the group into which Bede was himself settling nervously.

'We have,' said the therapist, a Mr Snow, 'a rule about Walkmans.'

The newcomer, smiling, a Maori lad not yet twenty, was slow to take the point. An argument of some politeness ensued, protracted and episodic, between the youth and the therapist, about standards of dress. Bede looked to Mr Salmon, the man of the dressing gown, and found him in a puzzling disarray. In light of the present spat it was as well that he was wearing a sturdy tweed jacket with leather patches at the elbow. But the folds of his neck and jowls were white with stubble. His moustache had lost its neatness. Not so his hair its chiming, silver ripples. He was doing something with a match to a cigarette holder, or vice versa.

'Even members of staff,' Mr Snow was saying, 'make efforts to look tidy in what for them is their second home. You can see that, Mr Salmon?'

'Quite.'

'Yes? Do you have any comment, Mr Salmon?'

Roused, there entered Mr Salmon's blue, patrician eyes the twin imps of malice and malice.

'Comment? Well, it occurs to me that at least one employee of this establishment gets around it as if in constant preparation for some sort of theatrical audition.'

This was understood by Mr Snow to be a reference to a Mr Shilling, his senior.

'Anything else, anyone, on the subject of dress?' he asked in an earnest enough attempt to close the subject. There was silence. 'In that case I will take the opportunity of confiding a suspicion I have. I am loath to do it. It is this. In my twenty years of work in this field, both here and in Canada, I have never before attempted to work with a group as lazy as this one. You take the cake. Internationally, too, at that. You have got to start taking your several recoveries seriously. I mean it. There's got to be some work done. Mr Salmon, we haven't heard much from you since your arrival.'

Bede thought there to be something ovine, something startled and aggrieved about Salmon's otherwise limpid glance at their leader.

'You've heard plenty from me, but not about me, is that what you mean, Snow?' Salmon's voice had a timbery echo Bede enjoyed. His eyes had a downward, Oriental cast, the skin about them much rucked-up and starry. His watery gaze had thus the look of an innocence widely tested, blue and hurtful to him. He put his cigarette holder to his mouth and bit on it with a sort of challenge; he was capable of severity.

'That's more or less what I meant, yes,' Snow admitted. 'I wondered if you were not in danger of taking too intellectual, too distanced a view of the events that brought you here.'

'Did you?' Salmon rumbled, as if any curiosity life had left him with could only be extended outward, to the matter of Snow's presence here himself, perhaps, come to that.

'Yes. Again, yes. And what I'm asking is'—holding his ground nicely—'don't you think it time, high time, you gave us the benefit of some of your own experience, experiences, knocking around bars and dives and cut-rate doctors' surgeries in Ponsonby and Willis Street and so on?'

Provocative, thought Bede.

'What do you mean, cut-rate? That was the point—some of my chaps got damned expensive.' Salmon seemed to consider himself justly enough rebuked. He pocketed his cigarette holder and spread his fingers before him, his elbows on his knees. Look, kids. 'It got very bad, I'll say that much.'

'How bad?' Bede.

Lunchtime was approaching. The rain had stopped. The wind had forgotten itself. They sat in a brown uniformity of shadow, listening. As in a snow-bound bunker, with the light dying and static crowding a last, vital message from the airwaves, Bede smelled bacon frying.

'She'd stripped the house of liquor. Our place faces the beach. What she didn't know was, in either direction along the high tide line I had plants. Out with the dog, that was the caper. North or south, it didn't matter, there were bottles buried. Then I would say, "Jean, you'd better ring Amy." Amy is her friend, she'd go and stay with Amy. And I'd play patience, for however long it took, order the grog from one of those big depots, home delivery. The last time I did this she sent a policeman. Time to pack it in he said, she wanted to come home, it had been a week. Now somehow or other—cravat, blazer—I got to see a quack in Hamilton. He was very interested. He took a cheque, it must have been a cheque. I came away with a script. The chemist gave me a jam jar full of footballs, hemis, Hemineurin, he was green with professional envy, I could have done with a handcart to get the stuff through the door and into the taxi.

Well, that Hemineurin, in that quantity, was the end of me, on that occasion. I bought another bottle on the way back to the house, just to begin the cure with. Our cab had done a few miles by this stage, the Samoan and I were agreed on that. When I came to in Intensive Care with my blood changed, his was the first voice I heard, days later of course. He was having some sort of bother with my cheque.'

FIVE

If bacon had been cooked there was no sign of it at lunch, nor of the ducks which came to the dining-room window in the morning, nor of Greg, whom Bede sought in connection with a duty he had been given. A soup made by the boyish, crippled cook seemed wildly adulterate: an odour, sweet, not unpleasant in itself, and which Bede associated with hotel corridors, was present in it.

As Bede was making tea for himself in the lounge, the sun came out. A man Bede had seen arriving in the van that morning joined him, minutes later, where he stood at the lounge windows.

'Your view's magic.'

'Isn't it. I see down there someone's building a log cabin or house.'

'I can see it too. Apple trees and some sort of old cart. He must be planning a tribe, he's making it big enough. My name's Michael Hart, by the way.'

Hart proffered his hand, frankly. It was done with a sort of skill. Bede shook it.

'No good skulking about friendless, place like this,' said Bede, obscurely pleased with himself.

Hart matched Bede in height. He was, too, of an average build. He was handsome in the long-lashed, dark-eyed way of the Black Irish. Perhaps to roughen his looks he wore his hair in an alarming, asymmetrical tangle.

At one o'clock the cook (known as Popeye because of his callipers and extreme emaciation) rang on a tumbler with a spoon, calling inside those patients who were taking advantage of the sunshine.

'The manager's away,' he called, 'and can't be with us this afternoon. He's left me with a list.' He had a clipboard from which he read chore details and names. 'Polly and Ann, no, Margaret: would you please round up all dessert plates. They seem to end up in the women's dorm.' Groans, laughter. 'Then come and see me and we'll have a look at the ovens now they're cool. Smith and Carlisle—where are you, men? . . .' and so on. Bede found him a bright enough character. At last he said, 'Ford, you've been fixed with the chapel I believe. Might pay you to go and have a word with Greg about cleaning materials. He's up with the pigs. Oh, and you can take Hart. Take heart and take . . . Never mind.'

Adjacent to the loading bay was a room in which Michael and Bede found gumboots of a passable fit. They trudged, though buoyant, up the long track to the piggery. The air was thin and chill and the sun still shone. The earth was a broken crust from which odours rose, refrigerated and dank.

The area in which Greg was working was cut into a knoll which kept it from the sun. Its concrete and wire construction seemed to cage a gloom. It was like a scene of sombre police discovery. This was a place of stoopings, of grim, forensic labellings. Bede imagined a string of cautionary bunting being hoisted ('All lift at once, now'), to allow the passage of some muddy, rigid mystery.

'You know anything about what needs doing in the chapel?' asked Bede.

Greg was laying dead rats in the bed of a wheelbarrow. He had a woolly, unsleek line of a dozen or so to transfer from a wall. They wore tiny, canine smiles.

'The windows,' said Greg. 'Outside and in. Vacuum. Squirt some scent about. I keep some gear in a locker for the purpose.'

'This,' said Bede, 'is Michael.'

'Hi, Mike. I could do with a smoke. Let's walk down through the pines.'

Greg stopped his work, pulled off his Swanndri and laid it across the rats. He wheeled the barrow from the enclosure and shut a rickety door. Feeling at the pocket in which he kept his tobacco, he led them off down the hill through a copse of pine seedlings. Some female patients waved, wagged pruning saws from a distance. They climbed the other side of the shallow declivity in which the pines, feathery and uniform, were being nurtured. At the top was a track made by cattle, novel and quaint at this height, in this place.

'I wanted to show you this.' Greg grinned over his shoulder.

Michael and Bede followed him down onto a grassy plateau. Below was the valley floor, level and fertile, and here a river had imposed its bright design. 'Curly,' said Michael. And so the water was, and tined, threads of its fabric parted by bleached, sheep-like stones in places.

'Yes,' said Greg. 'It's out of the way of things. I sometimes do a joint here. Haven't got one at the moment. Anyway, it's tricky during the week.'

'Where I was working,' said Hart, 'we had a test for it. Sometimes with our paranoiacs it was useful.'

'Where you were working?' Greg scowled.

'I'm training as a psychiatric nurse. I *was* in psychopedics.'

'Heavy.'

'It depends. I liked the old people, the relationships.'

'You're kidding.'

'Really. There's a lot that's hidden, that keeps surfacing wonderfully, Alzheimer's or no.'

They sat in fragrance and warmth. Michael offered them each a Camel. Greg accepted with a big man's shyness.

'We'd better wander back in a while,' said Bede.

'Here,' said Greg, 'is the key to that locker.'

'And where's the locker?'

'Chapel itself.'

Bede put the key in a pocket and lay back in the grass for a moment. He blinked at the clouds, at the dazzle at their edges. When he shut his eyes against their brightness, their vividity was reversed as in a photographic negative. Soon he felt the cool shadow of the sun's exclusion move down the length of his body. At this he felt a simple, animal disappointment.

Night. Letting his car gather speed, letting the car rattle, Bede is driving down a hill. Ahead is a corner, sharp. In time, soon, he must turn it. Let the car plunge, he can see where he must brake, he can see where he must turn. The camber of the road, meanwhile, is his sure, unerring track. His ride is pneumatic and quick. The wheel he holds vibrates minutely. He must turn it now. He brakes. There is a sudden change in the degree of things. The wheel vibrates for an instant with too little fineness. He feels through his thighs and buttocks the evacuation, the sudden expulsion from the car's chassis of a bulk, of a shape, swiftly. His grip begins the motion of a turn. But out of the downward pitch of the car's deceleration he can make no lateral curve. He holds, has hold of, impotence, of airy disengagement. He conceives of himself as a missile with infinite mass. Before he can brake further, even as he prepares a giant stab with his leg at the pedal, his thigh and calf enormous, a locking, a jamming, a sudden and concrete invalidation of his steering apparatus takes place with a bang. He has hit an invisible barrier, nether and immovable, and is being sucked skyward, upward, as if from behind.

Emerging on the other side of a tunnel, a vacuity, a hole in time, Bede had realised he was unhurt. He had been thrown clear of the car. His knuckles stung, had been grazed somehow. In a frost of broken glass, inverted, lay his vehicle. Its doors were agape. In its tumble along the road, end over end, the car had also ejected a seat. Where he crouched against a garage Bede could see it, a token of safety and order, out in the street in the beery light of streetlamps, a seat, sitting.

In the present again, Bede opened his eyes. The afternoon was cooling. Greg and Michael dozed. Here in the company of these good and quiet men it was sprung on him profoundly: that with all the white noise of personal disquiet hushed, made almost inaudible, there still buzzed in himself the desire to drink. A prompting to sex could not have been more frank. As to the accident, while it had everything to do with his being here in this treatment centre it had little to do with his drinking, its modes or degrees. And of his wife, his feelings for his wife? A seat sitting. He pictured her blank face. Its emotionless pallor was accusatory enough, enough for a dozen bitter marriages. To his burden of thirst, of craving, was added the nicety of guilt. He could only guess that she must regard him as being a very deficient, a very unpleasantly flawed sort of man.

SIX

The chapel's design did little more than hint at its function. It had tall windows at one end and a lectern at the other. Chairs were assembled in rows, in imitation of pews. Each chair bore a Good News bible. Bede found the locker to which Greg had given him the key. If it contained Windowlene and chamois, squeegee and scrim, it also contained, like missals, an orderly pile of *Penthouse* and a dozen coloured pornographic booklets from which the covers were missing.

'No wonder he keeps it locked,' said Bede.

'None. Afraid his Windowlene might walk.' Hart thumbed through one of the oddly anonymous magazines. 'Always intrigues me, the models in these kinds of things. I was in New York. They like the skinny junkie types because their cocks look bigger in the photos. You know, on the subject of the loss of self-respect, I've got a few thoughts. I feel more disgust and shame over a can of sardines I once shoplifted than I do about, oh, I don't know, a lot of other things. And I have days, whole days, when all I can recollect of my alcoholic conduct are the *faux pas*, the petty

208

borrowings, the sudden descents into sleep. Yet I've *lost* my self-respect as I might have lost a finger. It's gone, there's a gap, and I don't know where it might be.'

And this is the clinic which gives you back your finger? Bede instead asked something circumstantial.

'Yes,' continued Hart, 'they've got me all trussed up legally. I want to keep my job and complete my training, I must take "treatment".' He drew horns in the air with his fingers. 'And the Admissions Officer in town said they'd only treat me again, again, if I committed myself. The magistrate beamed and wished me luck. Not that he seemed to believe in all the spurious bullshit we went through, either.'

Bede had met men whose sharp, otherwise handsome features had been made the instruments of cunning. This was not quite so in Michael's case. Rather, Hart's voice suggested the threat of reaction, the sort of disengagement in which there is something of menace.

As clouds gathered beyond the chapel windows, Bede had time to clean all but the highest panes. A lecture would follow, then dinner. The light darkened bluely. Rain began to scratch its first, and audible, ticks and arrowheads on the other side of the glass.

Michael sat with Bede at dinner that evening. There was a seating plan, not much amended, which said he should. They were joined without fuss by Powell, a man in his sixties wearing a red tracksuit.

'You may smoke,' he said, making what Bede guessed to be a maritime joke. He set his plate down between theirs. Bede knew Powell to be a member of the staff, a counsellor. He introduced Hart accordingly.

'Not much of a night,' said Powell. 'Pity. I always go in on a Thursday, there's an AA meeting in town I've been attending since Adam was a grasshopper.'

'I've only just arrived,' said Hart. He was kindled, amused. 'But if you recommend it . . .'

'You'd like to come? Splendid. Eat your Olives-Berf. With any luck our numbers will be down and we can leave the van and take my car.' He peppered his food with vigour, not briefly. 'Only a month ago I was in Japan. Where you never have to season anything, once it's put before you. This looks nice, all the same.'

'Where did you go?' asked Hart.

'Kyoto. Spring. It was lovely. I met my wife there in spring.' Powell was wistful for a moment, blank. Then he remembered his knife and fork.

'I know Kyoto,' Michael said with care.

'Do you? We must talk in the car. As to that van, if the boss finds out the girls and boys have been eating chips in it . . .'

After coffee in the lounge with Michael and Greg, Bede went to the dormitory to change. It was empty. Only Greg's reading lamp burned. The ceiling here was low. The many sounds of the rain burdened the roof, blanketing and soporific. Bede heard a tinkling sound, as if of experiment or distillation, the rain at work. It came to Bede that he was happy here at the clinic.

He stood. He lifted his yellow transistor and clicked its tiny wheel.

'. . . even now. First reports say . . .' Bede heard, adjusting the tuner, '. . . is a local resident. Just repeating that: in the holiday town of Otaki not far from Wellington, a Ministry

210

of Transport officer is dead after shots were fired in a motor camp. The shooting began an hour ago and reports say it continues. A police spokesman says Armed Offenders Squad members . . .'

Bede switched off the radio. He changed his jeans for a dressier pair. He went to the lounge, a place he avoided at this hour in order not to be reminded that what was watched on the TV was, in theory, voted for. All the chairs were empty. A cartoon character boinged and spat. Bede sought the channel carrying news but a drama he sometimes watched was underway.

'Ready?' It was Hart. He wore a denim jacket lined with wool, his hands deep in the pockets.

'Yes. I'm wondering where old Powell keeps his car.'

'Search me.'

But a moment later Powell himself appeared. He made an impression on Bede fresher than that he had made at dinner. He was a slight man with high, raw cheekbones. His neat moustache was pronged. He wore a grey canvas jacket with roomy sleeves.

'Ah, here you are,' he said. 'I've brought our wheels to the front. If we set out now we should just about be there by midnight.'

A curious tension, thought Bede, existed in Powell between frailty and its maintenance. His age showed in his cheeks, their broken veins. Bede knew Powell jogged, not cosmetically. If he dyed his moustache it would be because his war against age was covert and opportunistic.

The car was an old Mercedes. Bede guessed it to be Powell's hobby. It smelled of machine-oil and leather. They rolled in darkness down a long, featureless track. From where he sat in the back, Bede could see only rain, an illuminated cone of aquatic insects, swarming.

When they had reached the main road, Powell driving in an unhurried, fluid style suggestive of training, perhaps military, Hart produced a bag of Minties.

'So you've been in Japan, Mr Hart?'

'I was there with my father, a diplomat, for my sixteenth birthday. We stayed in the Tawaraya Inn. It wasn't the first time I'd slept on a floor, but I couldn't get used to the absence of chairs.'

'Quite. I'd seen it after the war, you understand, was there again when I met my wife. She was Russian, matter of fact, a doctor. We loved it all and married there. Who'd have thought it.'

'Thought what?'

'I'd been a prisoner, you see. Burma.'

As Powell and Hart conversed, Bede remained silent. He took Powell, then, to be a widower. Rubbery, level, their ride was a ride through darkness, past lampposts lit by candles. As if selecting one of these as a cue, a flag of sanction, Powell spoke again.

'Their Burma. As the war drew to a close our conviction was that the Japs would have to surrender, that if they did that they'd butcher all our poor sods.'

He was an officer, thought Bede. Powell's eyes here followed a passing feature, a goat tethered close to the road, so that Bede saw his profile. He hid his chin like a boxer.

'A cop,' Bede said, 'has been shot. There's been shooting in Otaki,' as if, quite soberly, he had seen something stirring, someone gesturing, out in the blackness abreast of their car's dim headlights.

SEVEN

This was not to be the first AA meeting Bede had attended. He had gone to one drunk once. His mood on that occasion had been of a high, psychical lurching between tearfulness and anger, more poorly satirical than exploratory, and he had been ashamed of it afterward.

Some wet, yellow leaves stuck to a dampness—Bede stepped across them and was within a hall set up as if for some grim parish dance. The scents of Christmas lingered darkly, stalely, like those of unappealing cake. Indeed, a few paper streamers still remained in places, looped between rafters. Three men sat about a table set on trestles. There was a little scullery, too, where a well-dressed woman of middle age stacked sudsy cups and saucers beside a large, inverted teapot. She grinned at Powell in greeting; because someone at the table was speaking, she mouthed a silent welcome.

Bede knew enough to find a place with an ashtray. When he had settled into his chair he noticed with interest that Dr Lardwrist was one of the group. Of the two men remaining, one was small and simian and the other large, with a wide forehead and a complicated jawline. His skin shone with the closeness of his shave. He had a look of intelligence and reserve and, as the meeting got going, seemed always a little surprised, further amused, by its changes of gear, its formal evolution. His biceps moved in his thin, sporty jacket with a massive, global ease.

'We welcome our visitors,' said the little man who looked like a rhesus monkey. He had visible tufts on his cheeks where his razor had not reached. Nature itself was making a display of his nose and cheeks. They glowed sexually. 'My name is Brian and I'm an alcoholic. Each week, as you know, I visit the prison to carry the AA message. I'm always encouraged when prisoners have the heart to come out into the world, albeit briefly, to address with us their problems of alcoholism and drug dependence. Brendan here is with us tonight to listen, learn what he can, and perhaps share his own story with us. Meanwhile I'll call on Dr Lardwrist, if I may, to make a start. Doctor?'

At a rugby match, everything interested Bede but the game. In the present, however, he found the simple, human formulation of the meeting congenial. The high-coloured man who had spoken seemed to have chairmanship of a sort; his hand rested on a book as fat as a Bible. In a cheesy light redolent of dead festivity, Dr Lardwrist pulled himself into a semblance of polite posture. His spectacles were shillings of opacity for a second, then Bede glimpsed the watery intelligence behind them, blue, eyes in diffident search of something. They rested at last on Bede's, smiling a kind of apology.

'Well,' said the doctor, 'there's at least one young man present tonight I didn't expect to see here. Twenty years ago I would myself have laughed at the possibility of my ever venturing out on a night like this to attend an AA meeting. But there you are, stuff the weather, I'd go anywhere for a drink. Gin. That was my go. I bought it by the case, anywhere but here in town. Once I was signing, drafting a cheque with much artistic licence when the guy asked, you know, wasn't one case a day enough? Pills to start, pills to stop, a bottle hidden here, another there. I thought in terms of the *discipline* of addiction. Wow. But with the best will in the world, with all the skill of a memory trained in a study of medicine, I really ended by having a very sketchy idea of what I had taken, was taking. My car was a chemist shop. With all the stuff I was using, I had to invent a patient. There are certain drugs . . . that helped my drinking seem orderly and moderate. My surgery glowed like a dynamo. One night, two gents arrived. In no hurry, nice manners. But they weren't taking seats. You stop, they said. You clean this act right up. Because if you don't we'll take away your right to practise medicine.'

Lardwrist closed his eyes. He settled back in his chair. The woman Bede had seen in the scullery joined them quietly. The man with the handsome jaw, the criminal, had parted lips. The slant of his body in his chair, diagonal but bulky, was that of a skilled listener. If this was Lardwrist's party piece, Brendan, for one, had never before heard it.

'Believe me or believe me not,' said Lardwrist, 'all I had ever wanted to be was a doctor. And what had I become? These men threatened my very identity.' He opened his eyes. He looked at the ceiling. 'You know, there is a sense in which it is our personalities themselves which are threatened by our addictions. Our characters too, of course. I was lucky. I turned myself over to my colleagues. The light in my surgery went out that night. It stayed out for a good many months, terrible months. In the first weeks, among other things, but forming a sort of dissonant climax to a crescendo of lesser horrors, I had a heart attack. I dropped like a celebrity on the Hanmer Springs golf course. Had it not been so painful it might have been funny. My return to any sort of physical well-being was slow. So too my climb back into the old mental cockpit. But in this latter I found

AA indispensable. Today my attendance at its inconvenient little meetings is an essential part of my sobriety. I don't know why. AA, it seems, is more than the sum of its parts. There's a mechanism at work here we don't, we can't understand. Like men with sloping brows crowded about a bonfire in some Neanderthal winter of the spirit, we're here because we have to be. Let me just add that I am very grateful to be here tonight. I yield the floor, Mr Chairman. Thank you.'

Dr Lardwrist closed his eyes again. He straightened himself in his chair with his hands on his belly and sniffed, once, fastidiously. Bede saw that Brendan had enjoyed the performance, was not now sure he would like what might follow. The chairman spoke again.

'It's always refreshing to hear from you, Doctor. Perhaps at this point I might ask one of our visitors from Quest Clinic to say a few words. Perhaps the gentleman with the . . . ?'

Bede saw that the chairman was inviting him to speak. He had determined not to, of course. This decision, however, became suddenly irrelevant. In the present, newly engendered circumstances, only a second or two old, Bede felt a swift dissipation of his nervousness, his feeling of being a stranger to this group. It was moved aside like a screen to reveal a competence or skill Bede had forgotten himself to possess, an older thing than diffidence or pride. Composing his features into a smile of shrewdness, Bede spoke, if only in self-defence.

'With all due respect, I feel that I can do little more than introduce myself. My name is Bede and I'm an alcoholic.' There was a formal murmur of welcome. Bede took pleasure in this; it suited him to be speaking thus, and he continued. 'When I arrived at the clinic I talked with Dr Lardwrist about matters. I found it easy enough. I found it easy because I was less than frank with him. The fact of the matter is, a certain amount of bitterness was creeping into my thinking. I had tried to stop drinking and couldn't. I was only at my best at my work at the garage after a decent liquid lunch. I could remember, you see, a time when my drinking had been heavier. Perhaps it had also been less desperate.'

Bede felt what he had said formed a modest but finished bolus. But his audience wanted more. The chairman had not prepared himself to speak again so soon. There was a lull, a scratching rupture of continuity as the chairman's hand searched for a matchbox behind the big book in front of him on the table. Michael Hart took the opportunity of standing, restoring his chair to proximity to the table, and walking off in the direction of what looked like a lavatory, a door near the entrance. The chairman drew his matchbox toward himself across the table.

'Perhaps, then,' he said, 'our friend from ... Yes ... Brendan, was it?'

Brendan was ready enough to talk. As the chairman lit a fire in his pipe (a fire which seemed to spill, though green and oily, from the pipe's bowl like water), Brendan turned his palms to the company, knitted his fingers, and flexed and cracked his knuckles. Perhaps he would speak at length.

'I'm an alcoholic and my problem is Brendan.' The chairman had made a success of his pipe. He looked with alarmed, candid eyes at the speaker as if at some senior, more lushly-pelted ape. 'It is certainly a pleasure, a privilege to be asked to speak on my first visit to your group. I was born in Dublin, as my accent may tell you, at a very tender age, a good many years ago now. I guess I got up to all the usual childhood drinking pranks. By the time I was fifteen I was getting drinks all over. I had a mob of older brothers and had to be a part of their shenanigans. My eldest brother, Tommy, had me in a club for the boxing by the time I was sixteen. Of course, I was away at work b' then, a yard man with the coal and what have you. Get away to sea our Tommy had told me, and I did, I was off in the end, the worst thing I ever did, so far as the drinking was concerned, but not at first.'

Though Bede was interested in this, though it promised to provide an explanation as to what Brendan was doing in gaol, Bede felt there to be another, peripheral circumstance he should be attending. It might, he felt, alarm him if he could just bring it into consciousness. Brendan's clever facial mobility continued to tell a story, perhaps funny, in which there was more than a hint of sagacity. But Bede did not hear it. He was fitting a cigarette to his lips when it became clear to him why he was troubled.

He stood. He pocketed his cigarette. Like someone trying not to break a film projector's beam, Bede ducked with grace away from the table. He seemed to whisper a word of apology. His shoes knocked like clogs on the wooden floor as he crossed to the toilet door. He had a glimpse of the night without, felt its chill on his shoulder. He could smell, for an instant, foliage as he passed the hall's entrance. The door beside it swung inward. A light was on. The sole porcelain urinal chuckled and hissed at nothing.

There was a mirror, also vacant. Bede combed his hair at it. The Bede in the mirror smiled at Michael Hart's escape. He had strayed like an electron, blithely, obliquely. Bede lit his cigarette and inhaled with relish.

Reckoning that he had had time to pee, he opened the door and returned across the reverberative boards. Lit orangely from above, the faces and hands of those present had that waxen lambency Bede associated with the poker table. The folds of the chairman's pipe-smoke were plastic enough to have achieved blueness. Powell watched him as Bede resumed his seat. He returned Powell's look with a shrug, showing him empty hands: He's not in my pocket.

'When I was arrested for the robbery for which I'm now doing time,' Brendan was saying, 'I had no criminal record. I was living the life of an alcoholic seaman whose funds were running low. I had a room in a boarding-house in an unfamiliar city, an idle port. It seemed to me that shipping was at a standstill. In what policemen used to call a "disorderly house", I bought a pistol. Why? I had enemies. They followed me home to my crummy room, they populated my nights of crashing delirium, they came and went in whispers. They could only be bought with rum, appeased by the focus in a pistol's hateful eye. I was smoking a lot of dope, other people's ganja. My severance money was dwindling. I was mismanaging whores, I was mismanaging money. There was a bank near where we drank. The scale of the thing appealed to me, to what was left of my reason. By some queer chance I had seen that often its security video camera was not switched on. Picture it. I hadn't changed my clothes in weeks and wore one of those plastic, rubbery Groucho Marx masks with the glasses and big moustache, something I'd seen on TV. I was affable but firm. And just as if it was all a part of the game, as she piled up the money in front of me with every appearance of having done this sort of thing before, she switched the camera on with her toe, I saw her do it, as if adding some new touch or other to her makeup.'

Brendan grinned at the company. Powell leaned close to Bede.

'I'll have to do something unpleasant,' he whispered. 'I'll have to ring the police when this is over. They expect it.' He scowled.

Bede heard the whistle of a Zip from the scullery.

EIGHT

Michael Hart had left a note for Bede. It was written on a single sheet of paper torn from a sketch pad, folded once and left on Bede's bed.

Bede,
     Stoned, faceless, tremulous with the prescience of mescaline or datura, you might see this place as a clutch of radio components, all of crystal. It's aglow, this translucent chassis, with little worms of fire, with vortices of light, tiny and sharp. Your bloodstream steaming with Methedrine, you might paint it, you might draw it with an airbrush, this little city of glass. And what is its function? What does this pigmy metropolis of transparency and venous filaments do? It absorbs neuroses, it imbues itself with delusions.

Yours. Mine. Theirs.
I'm gone.
Michael.

Several days passed. One afternoon under an ashy, quilted sky, in a place where the air was saturate and a permanent dew clung in pearls to the gorse, Bede was helping Greg mend a fence.

'I heard at lunch,' said Greg, 'that they're bringing Michael back this afternoon.'

Hart arrived as they were having tea in the lounge. Two policemen brought him. They were curious as to the function of this place, its extent. Powell met them.

A doffing of hats; 'best-place-for-him' smiles of abdication; they went with the careful nonchalance of the observed back to their aliens' car.

What did Bede see?

Hart had the tousled hair of a fugitive. Bede got an impression of captivity, of identity smeared, of the operation on Hart of an ethos which was its own compulsion, *sans* proddings or handcuffs. Bede saw a handsome, cowed head, a shadowed face of some beauty on which the smile seemed irrelevant, futile. He saw this in the bright, forceful concentration of an instant.

Bede carried the image of Hart's profile, its stamp, into his counselling session with Mr Snow.

'Why do they bring him back? What's the point?' asked Bede.

Mr Snow was very fair. His face had a raw, veiny appearance. Winter's astringent air threatened to make it bleed. His skin seemed lit by irritations, a litmus paper on which were registered the stains of the inhospitable, the air, the very hour.

'The point is, and I'm sure you've already thought this through, that he has asked to be brought back. He did that when he had himself committed. Have you any idea what a menace that guy had become? Anyway, this is typical of you, your concerns are always exterior, never in there with yourself where they should be, given your more recent history. *You* are the lame duck for the time being and it's you you should be worried about, not him.'

'A menace?'

'They had to take some guns off him. But you know all that.'

'No. I hadn't heard.'

'He had a modest arsenal. Seen with the things at four in the morning, that sort of thing. Very nervous neighbours.'

'I believe he's something of an artist, a painter.'

'Won an Australasian prize. Look, we're here to talk about you. Have you written to your boss yet?'

'No.'

'You decided you would.'

'I've changed my mind.'

'So we're back to the drawing-board on that one. Mind if I make a note?'

'A weirdo, then. Him. Assembling, disassembling the instruments of death.'

'His winning entry was called "Glass of Water and Maiden". I hear they arrested someone this morning for a shooting in Otaki.'

'They stormed the house. They don't, you know, "storm" anything, they're very quiet. Mute, up trees.'

After dinner Bede moved his few things to a room he had been allocated. It was his own and small. There was a desk at which he might write those letters he dreaded because to each he must add this strange, remote address, an admission of defeat. His window looked out into that square of lawn and shrubbery where the little totem brooded. Night would soon immerse it.

'Knock out that wall and window, you've got my cell in Japan.' It was Hart.

'Really? Come in. Your cell?'

'Absolutely. I was in a Buddhist monastery for a while.'

'On what basis?'

'No basis. I was just there. The sound of two hands clapping, I suppose. My father had said he would send an airfare. Well, he took his time. So long, in fact, that I had time to get my head shaved.'

'The other monks did that?'

'No. A local barber. Outside our cells each morning one of the monks would make a fresh pattern in the sand, a new and careful pattern every morning with a rake. You must have seen it, that sort of thing, in photographs.'

'One doesn't think about the pattern being varied.'

'The design mutates, even for the godless, and I was godless enough.'

He stepped into the room. Hart had a face of a type, a face in which the cheeks were dominant. The images of two opposing hatchets, long and thin, seemed stitched into the skin. But there was about the modesty of Hart's spare physique something Bede thought he would like to embrace, to test the substance of. Hart had glamour, was a thing of attractive parts. He settled on Bede's bed with an untroubled, welcome discourtesy.

'Were you though, are we?' asked Bede. 'I wonder. Oh, I know, we're supposed to find it here, this spiritual life to which they urge us. But have you ever prayed?'

'I'll tell you. Do you mind if I smoke?'

Bede accepted a Camel. With an ashtray positioned near his thigh, Hart leaned back on the bed and into his own tumbling smoke. He rested on his elbows, his chest concave and shallow, his cigarette white beneath the dark asymmetry of his hair. He exhaled productively.

'I was returning from a detox ward,' Hart continued. 'I was going back to a cottage I rented on the beach. I'd been doing a little hunting, a little painting, before things caught up with me. There were pigs in the bush, I was equipping a studio, I had a lot riding on staying straight. My lady would stay, blah blah, I'd been promised some design work. There was a difference this time, or seemed to be. I had really tasted these very bitter lees. And been frightened. Dig this: it was all still an effort? This isn't a simple story. Suffice it to say that I wanted to stay sober, I had seen right to the bottom and, surprise, there *was* no bottom. So here I am on a bus, returning, and I ask myself what could possibly weaken my resolve in this matter. Understand the question, Bede. What circumstance? Then I twigged. It came to me. There was this one guy. Between us, between the two of us, drinking had always amounted to a sort of sacrament. I hadn't seen him in years. Imagine *his* turning up. After so long, after so pregnant an absence. So I asked, I asked Him, I asked God, "Is this what You've got planned? Is it?"'

'And did you get an answer?'

'My friend was waiting to meet the bus. I could have hit him. We only sat up until midnight. He drank two bottles of beer, and I, nothing, tea. But I don't think we ever got closer, were ever more clear-eyed and direct with one another than we were that night.'

Hart stood. Though, in a way, Hart's story was one of defeat, Bede felt for the moment a thrill of possibility, the intimation of what it might be to win, to flourish. For were they not young, was there not already something resembling friendship underway between them? Hart's shoulders radiated more than heat. The smile now making his cheeks two elongated dents of query revealed him to be a woodsman, a drinker at sobering springs. His teeth made that seem likely. Hart's smile had, too, the reassuring shape of scepticism. In this, Hart's caution struck Bede as being a function of his intelligence. For all their grace, Hart's shoulders were not broad. But he kept them present, spread. He made more room with them than the world had yet allowed them.

'So what frustrates us?' Bede asked. 'It seems to me that we have a fairly profound interest in states of mind, even in spiritual states. Where's the serenity?'

'I think of it as being a box, the box of entrapment in sequence, time's box. This frustrates us. Personally. But further to this, making really sure we don't get a good night's sleep, is our fear of nuclear winter, our memory of the death camps. For the time being, our collective nerve has been shaken.'

When Hart had gone Bede drew his curtains. Perhaps we love our own darkness. Reflecting on Hart's last remarks, Bede saw him as an artist whose interest in life was alchemical. There was no other word for it. Hart cast long shadows—at night. He brought his own mystery to the lesser mysteries of ammunition and firing-pin. And perhaps, like Kandinsky, he was the smocked manufacturer of his own pigments, a white-gowned chemist from whose deliquescent powders bloomed bloods, azure inks. He was certainly complex, had left something of his egregious congruence of mind and person behind him. But the forms of his cigarettes' blue and motile smoke, a series of steps or steppes erected in the air of Bede's still room, were already collapsing, were already becoming diffuse.

NINE

He had left his door open to clear the air. For a while he rested with his knuckles on the desk, looking at nothing, listening to a growing constriction in his chest, feeling a wind at his cheeks which did not exist.

Bede had a deep, private awareness of his asthma's ability to kill him. When it attacked it imposed a condition as dark as it was airless. It impeded. It numbed. It starved. Bede hated and dreaded it. Thus, when it threatened, was broadening the bands of its gluey inhibition, Bede had trained himself to take twenty milligrams of Prednisone. He knew it would keep him awake and alter his mood. Time spent on Prednisone was time apart, of a subtly elevated kind of perception. It was a drug Bede welcomed, like alcohol. But, like morphine, it deprived him of the proper recollection of its bliss, its many kinds of euphoria, variously enjoyed, and he looked forward to using it again. Prednisone. Months might pass when he need not take it.

When it became timely to resume its use, Bede was always a little glad. Its name suggested to Bede a holographic play of pastel geometries, the movement of thought across thought in gliding planes of transparency.

It had gone seven. The muted, tinny rattle of water beneath his window told him it rained, still, or again. He straightened. He must see Powell.

At a place in the passage where it darkened, became unfamiliar, intimated the possibility of trespass, Bede found Powell's door. He knocked. Powell wore a wine-coloured dressing gown in which seemed to move, at depth, other lustres and hues. Powell's room was his home. All of it. It had, therefore, a packed, orderly, complex character. And Powell was a travelled, well-read man. He had been reading in bed. A Penguin Evelyn Waugh lay face down on the carpet.

'Do you do much reading yourself, Bede?' he asked as he busied himself at a little Café Bar. 'Tea, coffee, chocolate? I can offer all three.'

'Tea, please. And sugars, two. Oh, I don't get much time for reading. Wilbur Smith, Laurens Van Der Post, that sort of thing. I think I'd like Africa.'

'*I* do. Hello, the sugar thing's gone bung. N'mind. There's more in the packet. Come to chat?'

'Not really. I need some medication. Lardwrist's left some tablets marked for me in the dispensary.'

Bede took one of two easy chairs. Here he felt a certain privilege, the pleasure of intimacy with things not his own. There were books, fish in a tank, the memorabilia of air force and cricket team. Powell brought their cups and sat down opposite Bede. In the present, abated light,

Powell's cheeks seemed broader, more Slavic than ever. But this appearance of breadth belonged to his cheeks alone. The dihedral of his moustache suggested balance, an equilibrium of tensions.

They stirred their respective drinks. Powell, smiling, seemed content with the silence between them. Surfaces: Bede found one on which to rest his cup. A thin, wheaten light: he had almost decided to give something a try.

'I have,' said Bede, 'misgivings.' And sounded to himself abrupt, surprised.

'Oh? About what?' asked Powell. His eyes winked on and off like running water. His glance bent upward as if from a shelter, a carapace.

'I want to put something to you. I've tried to decide what this place is. I've tried to decide if I belong in it. And my feeling is that I'm trapped behind barbed wire here. I feel I have unfinished business, out there in the world.'

'I believe you've a brother in Sydney.'

'And money from the sale of my bike. There's already trouble about my seeing my daughter. I could be in Aussie tomorrow.'

'Quite.'

'Aren't you going to try to dissuade me?'

'Me? I don't think so. It's never admitted, but there will always be people whose referral to these places is inappropriate. The question is, are you one of them. For me, the shame of all my past crimes keeps me sober. Where before it was a further reason to drink. I can't explain that. But because I'm sober I can exercise a choice.'

'Crimes?'

'Oh, yes, crimes. Social. Spiritual.' He smiled. They

228

were both being sly, taking advantage of the paucity of light. 'At least, that's how I've made myself think of them. You see, whatever they were they diminished me. They made me feel that any further protraction of my life would be wildly undeserved, prodigal.' Powell leaned backward, distancing himself from what he had just said. 'There's no good reason,' he continued, 'why psychology shouldn't turn an alcoholic into a perfectly ordinary social drinker. But how often does it do it? And can you do this for yourself?'

'Look. I'm not like these others. If it weren't for the car smash, the break-up of my marriage . . .'

'. . . you'd pass for someone else, someone without taint? I would have thought alcoholism, addiction to a sedative drug, a very ordinary, uninteresting failing. Indeed, it seems to have become quite a fashionable disease.' Under so expert, so easy a control, the annoyance in Powell's tone might be mistaken for gloom. 'I've watched you. There's something you're omitting, leaving out of the account.'

'What's that?'

'Your despair. It ticks away like a Geiger counter. It's all the time measuring what you see as being the failure of others to love you. Have you, by the way, made any friends here?'

'There's Hart. We were talking just now. He's friendly, interesting. Behind his back they say he's mad, dangerous.'

'And what do they say about you.'

Bede saw something, Bede glimpsed something he thought peculiarly his own. He moved to claim it.

'Shall I tell you?' he asked.

'Do.'

'Sweet fuck all.'

'You're right, of course. If they did, what do you think they'd say?'

'How should I know? That I'm touchy, deep?'

'Neither, I think. I'm guessing that you're actually seen as being rather amusing and satirical. *I* feel that you evince a somewhat aggressive nihilism. I don't much care for that. Who is your counsellor?'

'Mr Snow.'

'He's right for you. Loud socks. Please feel you can come to me too if you feel I can help in any way. You're not sitting on a set of keys, by any chance?'

Relating to more than the whereabouts of keys, Powell's smile was one of conjecture. Bede stood. He swept his lap with his hand. Perhaps he dislodged or cancelled crumbs of engagement, of intimacy. Then he turned, inspecting his chair without interest.

'Nope. No keys.'

'As you were. They were underneath my book. Shall we go?'

They went together to the dispensary.

Bede had taken his medication and was on, though not in, his bed reading when Snow made his final check at eleven.

'OK?' asked Snow.

'I'll probably not sleep.'

'Oh?'

'Some medication I'm on. Doctor's orders.'

'I'll be awake myself. I see you're trying the book I recommended. You'll find this hard to believe, but the Super thinks we've got a prowler.'

'A what? All the way out here? Where would he come from?'

Snow shrugged.

It was shortly after midnight when he returned. This time he sat. The skin of his forehead was taut and white as if once badly burned and mended now. He kneaded his pants where his penis might be.

'We've got a problem. I didn't want to mention it earlier, but Hart is missing.'

'Again?'

'He's becoming a fucking nuisance.'

Bede said nothing.

'He was in here earlier?'

Bede blinked his assent.

'Nothing eating him?'

'Nothing particular.'

It was as if Bede began a minor journey. He felt himself swung abroad by the action of the drug he had taken. The invisible vessel in which he rode got underway with a shudder of departure, of severance from the familiar. Yet the questions Snow posed, implied, warned of something. The medium on which Bede travelled seemed diminished, made palpably more shallow, by the news Snow brought.

'I'll phone the Super,' said Snow. 'He'll have instructions.'

The white of his blank, healed forehead burned an arc, a visible swathe, in the air as Snow went out. Bede closed his book. The slight, noiseless machinery of vigilance was in place, a clock of spinning baubles. It seemed to require of Bede some adjustment to himself, some action, perhaps, of circumspection and courage. His army-surplus jacket hung behind the door. Bede transferred his cigarettes and matches to one of its pockets, his handkerchief and Ventolin aerosol to another. (He had no keys. He had no flashlight.) Then he sat, to read again, this time at his desk, with a firm conviction of silliness, of his over-reaction to a threat not yet properly framed.

Mr Snow did not return. An hour passed. Bede made the occasional note, his pencil whispering.

Tetrahydroisoquiniline.

'Tetrahydroisoquiniline acts, it may be said, as a trigger.' Bede read these words with wonder. If what they said was so, his study was advancing. Two small bricks of knowledge, recent and lambent, he had nudged together to form a critical mass. He felt for a moment the pleasure of making a deft, personal synthesis of ideas. His hand strayed to where his cigarettes had lain on the desk. His mind returned to the room. He must stand in order to retrieve his cigarettes.

Bede could not doubt . . . that he heard a knock, three knocks, on his window. Unlikely. Clear. As real as objects, they spaced themselves like knots, like knobs, in time. Wooden, though their medium was glass, they were round and textured and aspired to having hue.

Bede's unstirring curtains told him nothing. He must open them. He did so. He saw only his own silhouette, the more massive features of his room reflected. Leaning closer to the glass only obscured him from himself. Dewy and bleached by the light, the fronds of the ferns beneath his window seemed undisturbed.

He donned his jacket. He freed his hair from his collar with snips of his fingers. Bede had been visited by hallucination before. The word 'visited' was apt. Hallucination had a talent for arrival, for interposition.

Bede knew it to be plausible, ordered and complete, the Ames-room of reason. On Methedrine and hashish once, for a full half-hour at a party, Bede had been part of a conversation for which he might have known the script. He would always remember the essential sanity of the experience. His power to anticipate speech, utterance, had been unassailable. He had played, too, the hilarious game of trying to deflect, derail, the force of this astonishing temporary power of his. But he had been in the presence of people whose every syllable and thread of clothing had a starkly elemental profundity, a nude vividity. He had known himself to be in a classical state of psychosis, prodigious in his powers of anticipation, omniscient. And emptied by it of guile.

But out here in the country some small, nocturnal commonplace was poking out its tongue at Bede. A farmer might explain it. Some anomaly of night and recent rain would account for the sounds at Bede's window. He could not believe in prowlers.

'Still up?'

Bede's fright went off like powder in his chest, the flash of photographer's lime.

'*Je*-sus. Christ. At *this* time of night. Cough or something, *please*, when you approach.'

It was Snow.

'Did I . . . ?'

'I've just heard noises, knocks.'

'Ah. So does the Super. Look, I thought I might check the out-buildings. In case I'm asked if I did when Hart fails to turn up. You follow?'

'Of course. I'll come too.'

'Why not. The rain's eased off. Follow me and I'll get myself a torch.'

They went to that room at the side of the building where weather-proof clothing was kept. This room was always for Bede like a somewhat cloacal air lock, a dank staging post *en route* to the outside world. They changed into gumboots. Snow selected a flashlight.

Bede could never get used to the completeness of darkness in the country. The night without lacked boundaries, sides. Snow's flashlight could touch none. It swayed about feebly finding the pendulous wires of a fence, a muddy, abandoned paint pot, the fleckless air itself.

They walked as far as the piggery. Here Bede remembered the rats, became conscious of his ankles. Soon, to Bede's relief, Snow led them away from the piggery. They began their return to the main building. Snow checked a tool shed, its medieval padlock. He scanned the fixed, flush door of another hut. Though the rain's cessation had left a residue of sound, of watery tinklings, all was intact and innocent of disturbance. The diffuse beam of Snow's flashlight, now bringing things close, now pushing them to remoteness, reached as often as not into vacancy.

'We'll have a fine day, you'll see,' said Snow. He had stopped again at a door. 'We haven't looked in here. I'd better open her up.'

They stood outside the facility's garage. Snow had keys. They entered through a door set in the door. There was room inside for two vans. Snow walked between them to a space behind. Here was a bench and a packing case or two.

'Ever drink meths?'

'No. Why?'

'Plenty of it in here. Untouched. Anyone drinking that inside would pong. Hello. Someone's left a knife out.' Snow picked it up from where it lay on a trestle, a carving-knife from the kitchen. From a spool on a shelf above, down to the level of the trestle hung some synthetic yellow twine. 'Someone has wanted some rope. Careless with our knife. Cook would have a fit.'

It was too long to pocket. Bede carried it instead. Snow locked the door in the door and they left the garage. They removed their gumboots in the room they had taken them from. They carried their shoes on into the main building. In the dining room, at what would be Bede's place at breakfast, he left the carving knife.

They reached the patients' kitchen. Its hatch's slide was up, as always, providing a window on the darkness of the lounge.

'Well,' said Snow, 'there's no sign of our friend.'

'Or anyone else.'

'I'll just check the lounge.'

Bede wondered why Snow had not yet done this. Snow extinguished his flashlight and switched the kitchen light on.

A dog with one leg missing had once struck Bede as being grotesque. To study the face of a child hanging upside down in a playground . . . This shift in perception was for Bede radical, unwelcome. In this regard, what perverse imagining could be more disturbing than that of an elderly woman walking on her hands and knees *across a ceiling*?

Here in the lounge, it occurred to Bede that Hart was *up* on something, was standing perhaps on a chair. Bede saw only the shins of Hart's jeans at first. But why should they be turning thus so slowly together, legs on a slow turntable?

Hart was standing in, on, vacancy. His loins were a clothed, lumpy representation of an erection. On a level with his waist, saintly, Hart's hands were extended slightly as if to intercept a bouncing ball. They had been at his throat, at the taut, inflexible rope about his neck, and were sticky with tea-coloured blood, what might be blood. They had been unevenly basted. Hart's neck and throat were the pinks and mauves of a faded cookbook photograph, a sun-blenched butcher's chart. His body turned, could just be said to twirl, a thing in water, its nature obscure, and moved by an almost imperceptible wash. It conveyed a disappointment, seemed frankly to admit its inability to reach, step down to, alight upon, the floor.

The sign which said QUEST CLINIC gathered light like dust in the shadow. Its aluminium letters seemed laminations, pairings of line and contour not quite matched. The geraniums near the entrance had achieved a degree of colour by the time the police arrived. They came shortly after dawn. Mr Snow was there to meet them; Bede stood near him. A thing of details and edges, the police car had a decked, betackled appearance. If as sombre as its surroundings it had at least the appeal of having been recently in motion. Two uniforms—two sets or examples of an exterior reality—climbed out of the car. The faces beneath the peaked caps were youthful. They evinced and invited interest. They would pass, Bede guessed, that test which was to come, of disengagement of death from the tangle of life, of extrication.

The policemen removed their caps. Now they could be distinguished. One of them winked at Bede. He was of

Bede's age, had Bede's complexion. His eye retained the limpidity of newness, would take some sullying yet. His wink meant simply, Good morning, A bad business. For the moment there existed no one this policeman had ever suspected of error.

'The mortuary van is on its way' and 'You've touched nothing?'—Bede heard these things as if from over a wall.

He went to his room. Drawing them tight with a sort of desperation, Bede retied his laces. He took his wallet and bankbook from the desk. He put them in a pocket of his jacket, a jacket in which were pockets for hiding maps. He lay down on his bed. In spite of the Prednisone he had taken . . .

When Bede woke he could not find his watch. He realised he wore it. It showed the bountiful addition of a wedge, a slice of time. It was ten o'clock, still morning, and his room was full of light, pervasive, scalding.

He was very much outside when he stopped walking. The clinic's buildings were behind him. He stood on a grassy slope with a view of the valley. In a distant saucer of habitations blossom and smoke crowded to completion the log cabin Bede had watched being constructed.

He had been too much inside. He smoked at work. He lay on his back beneath cars, his cigarette nodding like a beak when he spoke, when he called for tools to be passed. Asked his opinion of anything, pushing his palms down his thighs because they were soiled, he was full enough of charm and waspish frankness. But he practised his trade in darkness. To stand at the garage door on a Friday night, to sit with the lads over a carton of Foster's beer, was to strip as if for a swim. He was naked then, unarmed. After rain the road outside their garage might glisten. Though the larger brightness of neon was reflected, the pavement's surface had its own patina of light, of tiny lights. Perhaps it was light he sought. Or air. Or the absence of certain things. His future drinking would take place in the sun. On patios and terraces, on steps and in airy cloisters, anywhere that was lofty, he would toast strange harbours. The grime beneath his nails, as blue as his overalls, had been a source of pride. Let his pride take him abroad.

To fix the thrill of the moment, to freeze its evanescence, Bede must act. He straightened. He stretched up on his toes. Like a diver testing the end of a board, he balanced there, rocking. He formulated intent. His body dropped through the length, the line of its height, he assumed for an instant a crouch—and he was off.

He was running downhill. He was running away from Quest Clinic. He was running before the sun.

He found it easy. As in a dream of running, it was very like flight. He might run to Sydney. The narrow carpet of his shadow pushed ahead of him, took objects large and small in its silent, skittering, tide. Noiselessly, closely, it conquered, it mastered terrain. Losing nothing of itself, it rippled across a grate for stopping cattle.

The path, the track, became firmer. It was summer he was cleaving, the very season itself, its unimpeding presence. As if brought forward like a date, advanced on the calendar like some fixture of release and celebration, today brought attainment. Bede moved swiftly through its bright prematurity. He was conscious of his body, his body's stature.

He impelled it with the modest force of his will. He felt

elevated and broad. Carrying a wide, inclusive vision, he sped between fences. To his left was a gorsey bank, to his right the pines and willows which hid a river. Bede could see the rise which would bring him to the road. The air was sweet and warm. It was pooled, dammed-up in places, taking on the wobble of hotness. Ahead, where he was aimed, was the focus of its sweetness, the struts of a wooden sign and streak of asphalt, bending like allure in a captive heat.

Bede heard, at no great distance, the tall, buffeting horn of a logging truck.